# Who Kissed Me in the Dark

**Ruskin Bond** has been writing for over sixty years, and now has over 120 titles in print—novels, collections of short stories, poetry, essays, anthologies and books for children. His first novel, *The Room on the Roof*, received the prestigious John Llewellyn Rhys Prize in 1957. He has also received the Padma Shri (1999), the Padma Bhushan (2014) and two awards from Sahitya Akademi—one for his short stories and another for his writings for children. In 2012, the Delhi government gave him its Lifetime Achievement Award.

Born in 1934, Ruskin Bond grew up in Jamnagar, Shimla, New Delhi and Dehradun. Apart from three years in the UK, he has spent all his life in India, and now lives in Mussoorie with his adopted family.

# RUSKIN BOND

*Who Kissed Me in the Dark*

RUPA

Published by
Rupa Publications India Pvt. Ltd 2017
7/16, Ansari Road, Daryaganj
New Delhi 110002

*Sales centres:*
Allahabad Bengaluru Chennai
Hyderabad Jaipur Kathmandu
Kolkata Mumbai

ISBN: 978-81-291-3594-0

First impression 2017

10 9 8 7 6 5 4 3 2 1

# Contents

# Introduction

The hill stations of India, many of them settled by the British, served a number of purposes once upon a time. Some were summer capitals, others were administrative centres with strategic importance. Many were beautifully scenic spots that held out an inviting hand to those tired from the heat of the plains. Today, the hill stations have grown and changed quite remarkably. Where there were green hills now there are rows of houses and hotels and restaurants. The streets are clogged with cars bringing in holidaymakers from the plains. The noise from the car horns and traffic drown out the softer sounds of nature—the wind rushing through the trees and the bird calls. But for long-time residents, there are some stories and memories that remain thankfully unchanged.

Mussoorie even now is full of beauty. I have lived in a couple of houses here, before making my home in the higher reaches of Landour. In all these years, I have heard and read a bit of the history and the legends that have grown around this town. Some stories are official accounts of how the hill station came to be. Some others are legends that have grown around long-deceased residents. Yet others are about those who are said to have met their Maker and yet appear in disconcerting fashion now and then, specially to the faint-hearted. And some other stories are those that I have experienced in my life. From my childhood that was more in the Doon valley to days of my youth when I decided to move to Mussoorie and now, there is a lot that has happened.

Among these people is that unknown girl who once kissed me in the dark. The lights had gone out, there was some amount of chaos all around and someone kissed me and disappeared. It's a nice mystery to have in one's life, I feel. I can wonder who it was and there lies a tale in the not knowing. Once upon a time, the year of the kissing was quite famous. But that was well before my time. The accounts of those who met happily or tragically at this time and of those who stayed on and those who came by many years later looking for them are vivid and dramatic.

I have collected a few stories here that talk about life in this most wonderful hill station. There are also stories of those who may well have lived here, so perfect a spot it is for stories to grow. Despite the bone-chilling cold winter nights or the times storms carry away the roof, there is unlikely to ever be a place that I would rather call home than this queen of the hills.

Ruskin Bond

# Frogs in the Fountain

Marigolds grew almost everywhere in our beautiful country, and they are constantly in demand—at festivals, marriages, religious ceremonies, arrivals and departures, functions of all kinds. If you happen to be a guest of honour on a public occasion, be prepared to be smothered in garlands of marigolds. I am a little wary of these welcoming garlands because on one occasion a slumbering bee, nestling between the petals, flew out and stung me under my chin. It made for a very short speech.

When I told young Gautam about this incident, he asked, 'Is that how you got your double chin?'

Actually the double chin came from my grandmother, who was a large, generously proportioned lady with a number of chins. Gautam and his sister Shrishti like to play with my double chin, but I would never have dared touch my old Granny on her chin or anywhere else. She was a stern, reserved woman, with a strict Victorian upbringing, who believed that little boys should speak only when spoken to.

She fed us reasonably well—she kept a great khansama—but she did not believe in second helpings, with the result that I spent the rest of my life indulging in second helpings.

Two mutton koftas were all that I was allowed with my plate of rice. I liked koftas—still do—and it was painful for a small boy to have to stop at two. Now that I am a grown man with an independent source of income, I help myself to four! Who can stop me?

Dr Bhist, who drops in to see me once a year, remarked that I looked overweight and that I should cut down on my food intake.

'What did you have for lunch?' he asked.

'Kofta curry and rice.'

'How much rice?'

'Just two small helpings.'

'And how many koftas?'

'Only four.'

'Don't have more than two,' he advised.

'Yes, Granny,' I said.

Dr Bhist gave me a puzzled look.

'Sorry,' I said, 'I thought you were my grandmother.'

Now he thinks I've got Alzheimer's.

'Talking of marigolds, Granny surrounded her house with them, as she believed they kept snakes away. Apparently, snakes do not like their pungent aroma. I, too, believed in this folklore until I was told (by an expert on reptiles) that snakes do not have a strong sense of smell and would be impervious to the scent of flowers or other odours. Maybe so, but I don't recall ever seeing a snake in Granny's garden, although I did see them elsewhere. However, we did have plenty of frogs, thanks to the disused fountain installed by my grandfather but neglected after his death.

The fountain hadn't functioned for a couple of years, but the little reservoir in which it stood had filled up with rain water and was now covered with water lilies.

One day, after an expedition to the Canal Head Works, I brought home some small fish in a bucket and introduced them to the lily pond. I hadn't paid much attention to the tadpoles swimming around in the bucket.

Well, the fish died as they were used to fresh running water and not stagnant water; but the tadpoles did *very* well, and before long we had frogs leaping all over the place. Very soon the frogs multiplied. They would come into the verandah at night and keep us awake with their incessant singing and warbling.

'I can't sleep a wink,' complained Aunt Mabel, who was very sensitive to noise and allergic to choirs made up entirely of bass singers.

'They're serenading you,' I said. It was a long time since anyone had serenaded Aunt Mabel, a confirmed spinster in her early forties.

'They'll go *away* once the rains finish,' said Granny hopefully. But they did not go away. One day, screams came from the bathroom—Aunt Mabel screaming for help! Granny, the khansama and I ran to her aid, and discovered that the cause of her distress was a large frog swimming around in the potty.

I pulled the flush chain. There was a loud gurgling sound, a combination of frog and flush, and out jumped the frog straight into Aunt Mabel's arms. She left for Lucknow that day, saying she would be safer in a zoo, where her cousin was the superintendent.

Well, Granny hired some labourers to empty the lily pond and round up as many frogs as they could. They were put into baskets and taken to some mysterious destination.

'Perhaps they've been exported to China,' I mused, 'or even to France. They eat frogs there, don't they?'

'Only the legs,' said Granny.

But they hadn't been exported. The khansama told me later that the baskets had been opened and dumped near a pond behind the railway station and before long they were all over the station waiting rooms and platforms, until the stationmaster had a brilliant idea. He had the frogs rounded up by a number of street urchins who wanted to make a little pocket money; he then had them packed firmly into several well-ventilated boxes.

The crates were labelled 'To Lucknow Zoo—Attn: Superintendent sahib', and dispatched as a free gift.

'A zoo is the best place for creatures great and small,' opined our philosophical stationmaster, who had previously sent them a consignment of stray station dogs.

Strangely enough, Aunt Mabel would have preferred a crate of frogs to a bouquet of flowers. She was allergic to flowers. Apparently the pollen brought on sneezing fits.

A fear of flowers is called anthophobia, and Aunt Mabel suffered from it. She lived in constant terror of flowers. An innocent pansy made her think of the devil; a snapdragon reminded her of real dragons; the spear-like leaves of the iris were as real spears to her; and the golden rod sent shivers down her spine. The ones that made her sneeze the most were hollyhock, cosmos, calendula, daisies of all kinds and chrysanthemums.

It was more than an allergy, it was an irrational but very real fear of flowers. Their very names terrified her. If I shouted 'thunder lily!' she would turn pale and tremble like a leaf. If I whispered 'gladioli', she would let out a shriek. If I said 'dandelion!' she would get a rash. And if I exclaimed 'convolvulus!' she'd go into convulsions.

Small boys can be cruel, especially to aunts, and I was no exception. But teasing Aunt Mabel with flowers had a limited appeal for me. Instead, I used them for blackmail. If I needed money for the cinema, I would take Aunt Mabel a bunch of larkspur or candytuft. She would turn pale at my approach, push me out of her room, and hurriedly give me the price of a cinema ticket.

In Lucknow, she lived in a flat and was able to keep flowers at bay. But in Dehra she had to put up with Granny's garden, and Granny had no intention of doing away with her flower garden. After all, she was acknowledged to have the most luxuriant display of sweet peas in town. Also Aunt Mabel stayed indoors most of the time, venturing out only in a tonga. She felt quite safe in Paltan Bazaar where there were no flowers apart from the cauliflowers on sale in the sabzi mandi, and even these she avoided.

So engraved was my aunt's phobia that she made everyone in the family promise that when she died there would be no flowers at her funeral. However, she did not really trust us to carry out her wishes, and this may have been the reason why she left India and chose to settle in Arizona, in an area where even the cacti had a hard time surviving. She'd found happiness at last.

I, on the other hand, cannot live without flowers. A little vase of bright yellow and orange nasturtiums rests on the corner of my desk, and every now and then I look up to refresh my eyes and mind by gazing at them. I have never been able to afford a large house with a garden (like Granny's, which was sold when she died) but I grow geraniums in my window and nasturtiums on the roof, and in the spring I throw cosmos seed on the hillside and some of them come up and reward me and others with autumn flowers.

Of course we all have our phobias, and some of the most interesting include bacteriophobia, a fear of germs; mysophobia, a fear of dirt (I knew someone who would wash her hands thirty to forty times a day, even when she was at home and unoccupied); xenophobia, a fear of strangers; nyctophobia, a fear of darkness; agoraphobia, a fear of open spaces. The trouble is, most of us—men especially—hate to admit being afraid of anything. This fear of showing fear is a phobia in itself. The word for it is phobophobia.

My own particular phobia is a fear of lifts. As far as possible I will avoid entering a building where it is necessary to use a lift. If I do go in, I take the stairs. On one occasion I was incarcerated in a five-star hotel where there was no staircase. My room was on the seventeenth floor. I was forced to use the fire escape! Now you know why I prefer to stay at the India International Centre whenever I'm in New Delhi: not because I have any intellectual pretensions, but because the building (god bless the architect) has only two floors.

Perhaps the best way of dealing with a phobia is to give in to it, admit it, tell everyone about your weakness, and enlist their support. I can tell people that I'm afraid of lifts. As most fellow humans are sympathetic by nature, they crowd into the lift to keep me company, and press all the right buttons something I have never been able to do successfully in lifts, on cell phones or with ladies' corsets.

Company in a lift always makes me feel much better. I know I won't be alone when it crashes.

# Grandfather's Many Faces

Grandfathers had many gifts, but perhaps the most unusual—and at times startling—was his ability to disguise himself and take on the persona of another person, often a street vendor or carpenter or washerman; someone he had seen around for some time, and whose habits and characteristics he had studied.

His normal attire was that of the average Anglo-Indian or Englishman—bush shirt, khaki shorts, occasionally a solo topee or sun helmet—but if you rummaged through his cupboards you would find a strange assortment of garments: dhotis, lungis, pyjamas, embroidered shirts, colourful turbans... He could be a Maharaja one day, a beggar the next. Yes, he even had a brass begging bowl, but he used it only once, just to see if he could pass himself off as a bent-double beggar hobbling through the bazaar. He wasn't recognized but he had to admit that begging was a most difficult art.

'You have to be on the street all day and in all weather,' he told me that day. 'You have to be polite to everyone—no beggar succeeds by being rude! You have to be alert at all times. It's a hard work, believe me. I wouldn't advise anyone to take up begging as a profession.'

Grandfather really liked to get the 'feel' of someone else's occupation or lifestyle. And he enjoyed playing tricks on his friends and relatives.

Grandmother loved bargaining with shopkeepers and vendors of all kinds. She would boast that she could get the better of most men when it came to haggling over the price of onions or cloth or baskets or buttons... Until one day the sabziwala, a wandering vegetable seller who carried a basket of fruit and vegetables on his head, spent an hour on the verandah arguing with Granny over the price of various items before finally selling her what she wanted.

Later that day, Grandfather confronted Granny and insisted on knowing why she had paid extra for tomatoes and green chillies. 'Far more than you'd have paid in the bazaar,' he said.

'How do you know what I paid him?' asked Granny.

'Because here's the ten-rupee note you gave me,' said Grandfather, handing hack her money. 'I changed into something suitable and borrowed the sabziwala's basket for an hour!'

Grandfather never used make-up. He had a healthy tan, and with the help of a false moustache or beard, and a change of hairstyle, could become anyone he wanted to be.

For my amusement, he became a tonga-wala; that is, the driver of a pony-drawn buggy, a common form of conveyance in the days of my boyhood.

Grandfather borrowed a tonga from one of his cronies, and took me for a brisk and eventful ride around the town. On our way we picked up the odd customer and earned a few rupees which were dutifully handed over to the tonga owner at the end of the day. We picked up Dr Bisht, our local doctor, who failed to recognize him. But of course I was the giveaway. 'And what are *you* doing here?' asked the good doctor. 'Shouldn't you be in school?'

'I'm just helping Grandfather,' I replied. 'It's part of my science project.' Dr Bisht then took a second look at Grandfather and burst out laughing; he also insisted on a free ride.

On one occasion Grandfather drove Granny to the bank without her recognizing him. And that too in a tonga with a white pony. Granny was superstitious about white ponies and avoided them as far as possible. But Grandfather, in his tonga driver's disguise, persuaded her that his white pony was the best-behaved little pony in the world; and so it was, under his artful guidance. As a result, Granny lost her fear of white ponies.

One winter the Gemini Circus cane to our small north Indian town, and set up its tents on the old parade ground. Grandfather, who liked circuses and circus people, soon made friends with all the show folk—the owner, the ring-master, the lion-tamer, the pony riders, clowns, trapeze artistes and acrobats. He told me that as a boy he'd always wanted to join a circus, preferably as an animal trainer or ringmaster, but his parents had persuaded him to become an engine-driver instead.

Driving an engine must be fun,' I said.

'Yes, but lions are safer,' said Grandfather. And he used his friendship with the circus folk to get free passes for me, my cousin Melanie, and my small friend Gautam who lived next door.

'Aren't you coming with us?' I asked Grandfather. 'I'll be there,' he said. 'I'll be with my friends. See if you can spot me!'

We were convinced that Grandfather was going to adopt one of his disguises and take part in the evening's entertainment. So for Melanie, Gautam and me the evening turned out to be a guessing game.

We were enthralled by the show's highlights—the tigers going through their drill, the beautiful young men and women on the flying trapeze, the daring motorcyclist bursting through a hoop of fire, the jugglers and clowns—but we kept trying to see if we could recognize Grandfather among the performers. We couldn't make too much of a noise because in the row behind us sat some of the town's senior citizens—the mayor, a turbaned Maharaja, a formally dressed Englishman with a military bearing, a couple of nuns, and Gautam's class teacher— but we kept up our chatter for most of the show.

'Is your Grandfather the lion tamer?' asked Gautam.

'I don't think so,' I said. 'He hasn't had any practise with lions. He's better with tigers!' But there was someone else in charge of the tigers.

'He could be one of the jugglers,' said Melanie.

'He's taller than the jugglers,' I said.

Gautam made an inspired guess: 'Maybe he's the bearded lady!'

We looked hard and long at the bearded lady when she came to our side of the ring. She waved to us in a friendly manner, and Gautam called out, 'Excuse me, are you Ruskin's grandfather?'

'No, dear,' she replied with a deep laugh. 'I'm his girlfriend!'

And she skipped away to another part of the ring.

A clown came up to us and made funny faces.

'Are *you* Grandfather?' asked Melanie.

But he just grinned, somersaulted backwards, and went about his funny business.

'I give up,' said Melanie. 'Unless he's the dancing bear.'

'It's a real bear,' said Gautam. 'Just look at those claws!'

The bear looked real enough. So did the lion, though a trifle mangy. And the tigers looked tigerish.

We went home convinced that Grandfather hadn't been there at all.

'So did you enjoy the circus!' he asked, when he sat down to dinner late that evening.

'Yes, but you weren't there,' I complained. And we took a close look at everyone—including the bearded lady!'

'Oh, I was there all right,' said Grandfather. 'I was sitting just behind you. But you were too absorbed in the circus and the performers to notice the audience. I was that smart-looking Englishman in the suit and tie, sitting between the Maharaja and the nuns. I thought I'd just be myself for a change!'

# On Foot with Faith

All my life I've been a walking person. To this day, I have neither owned nor driven a car, bus, tractor, aeroplane, motor-boat, scooter, truck, or steam-roller. Forced to make a choice, I would drive a steam-roller, because of its slow but solid progress and unhurried finality.

In my early teens, I did for a brief period ride a bicycle, until I rode into a bullock cart and broke my arm; the accident only serving to underline my unsuitability for wheeled conveyance or any conveyance that is likely to take my feet off the ground. Although dreamy and absent-minded, I have never walked into a bullock cart.

Perhaps there is something to be said for sun signs. Mine being Taurus, I have, like the bull, always stayed close to grass, and have lived my life at my own leisurely pace, only being stirred into furious activity when goaded beyond endurance. I have every sympathy for bulls and none for bull-fighters.

I was born in the Kasauli Military Hospital in 1934, and was baptised in the little Anglican church which still stands in this hill station. My father had done his schooling at the Lawrence Royal Military School, at Sanwar, a few miles away, but he had gone into 'tea' and then teaching, and at the time I was born, he was out of a job.

But my earliest memories are not of Kasauli, for we left when I was two or three months old; they are of Jamnagar, a small state in coastal Kathiawar, where my father took a job as English tutor to several young princes and princesses. This was in the tradition of Forster and Ackerley, but my father did not have literary ambitions, although after his death I was to come across a notebook filled with love poems addressed to my mother, presumably while they were courting.

This was where the walking really began, because Jamnagar was full of palaces and spacious lawns and gardens. And by the time I was three, I was exploring much of this territory on my own, with the result that I encountered my first cobra who, instead of striking me dead as the best fictional cobras are supposed to do, allowed me to pass.

Living as he did so close to the ground, and sensitive to every footfall, that intelligent snake must have known instinctively that I presented no threat, that I was just a small human discovering the use of his legs. Envious of the snake's swift gliding movements, I went indoors and tried crawling about on my belly, but I wasn't much good at it. Legs were better.

Amongst my father's pupils in one of these small states were three beautiful princesses. One of them was about my age, but the other two were older, and they were the ones at whose feet I worshipped. I think I was four or five when I had this crush on two 'older' girls—eight and ten respectively.

At first I wasn't sure that they were girls, because they always wore jackets and trousers and kept their hair quite short. But my father told me they were girls, and he never lied to me.

My father's schoolroom and our own living quarters were located in one of the older palaces, situated in the midst of a veritable jungle of a garden. Here I could roam to my heart's content, amongst marigolds and cosmos growing rampant in the long grass. An ayah or a bearer was often sent post-haste after me, to tell me to beware of snakes and scorpions.

One of the books read to me as a child was a work called *Little Henry and His Bearer*, in which little Henry converts his servant to Christianity. I'm afraid something rather different happened to me. My ayah, bless her soul, taught me to eat paan and other forbidden delights from the bazaar, while the bearer taught me to abuse in choice Hindustani—an attribute that has stood me in good stead over the years.

Neither of my parents was overly religious, and religious tracts came my way far less frequently than they do today (*Little Henry* was a gift from a distant aunt). Today everyone seems to feel I have a soul worth saving, whereas when I was a boy, I was left severely alone by both preachers and adults. In fact the only time I felt threatened by religion was a few years later when, visiting the aunt I have mentioned, I happened to fall down her steps and sprain my ankle. She gave me a triumphant look and said, 'See what happens when you don't go to church!'

My father was a good man. He taught me to read and write long before I started going to school, although it's true to say that I first learned to read upside down. This happened because I would sit on a stool in front of the three princesses watching them read and write, and so the view I had of them books was an upside-down one; I still read that way occasionally, especially when a book begins to get boring.

My mother was at least twelve years younger than my father, and liked going out to parties and dances. She was quite happy to leave me in the care of the ayah and bearer and other servants. I had no objection to the arrangement. The servants indulged me, and so did my father, bringing me books, toys, comics, chocolates and of course stamps, when he returned from visits to Bombay.

Walking along the beach, collecting seashells, I got into the habit of staring hard at the ground, a habit which has stayed with me all my life. Apart from helping my thought processes, it also results in my picking up odd objects—coins, keys, broken bangles, marbles, pens, bits of crockery, pretty stones, ladybirds, feathers, snail-shells, seashells! Occasionally, of course, this habit results in my walking some way past my destination (if I happen to have one). And why not? It simply means discovering a new and different destination, sights and sounds that I might not have experienced had I concluded my walk exactly where it was supposed to end. And I am not looking at the ground all the time. Sensitive like the snake to approaching footfalls, I look up from time to time to examine the faces of passers-by just in case they have something they wish to say to me.

A bird singing in a bush or tree has my immediate attention; so does any unfamiliar flower or plant, particularly if it grows in an unusual place such as a crack in a wall or rooftop, or in a yard full of junk where I once found a rose bush blooming on the roof of an old Ford car.

There are other kinds of walks that I shall come to later but it wasn't until I came to Dehra and my grandmother's house that I really found my feet as a walker.

In 1939, when World War II broke out, my father joined the RAF, and my mother and I went to stay with her mother in Dehradun, while my father found himself in a tent on the outskirts of Delhi.

It took two or three days by train from Jamnagar to Dehradun, but trains were not quite as crowded then as they are today and, provided no one got sick, a long train journey was something of an extended picnic, with halts at quaint little stations, railway meals in abundance brought by waiters in smart uniforms, an ever-changing landscape, bridges over mighty rivers, forest, desert, farmland, everything sun-drenched, the air clear and unpolluted except when dust storms swept across the plains. Bottled drinks were a rarity then, the occasional lemonade or 'Vimto' being the only aerated soft drink, apart from soda water which was always available for whisky pegs. We made our own orange juice or lime juice, and took it with us.

By journey's end we were wilting and soot-covered, but Dehra's bracing winter climate soon brought us back to life.

Scarlet poinsettia leaves and trailing bougainvillaea adorned the garden walls, while in the compounds grew mangoes, lichis, papayas, guavas, and lemons large and small. It was a popular place for retiring Anglo-Indians, and my maternal grandfather, after retiring from the Railways, had built a neat, compact bungalow on Old Survey Road. There it stands today, unchanged except in ownership. Dehra was a small, quiet, garden town, only parts of which are still recognizable now, forty years after

I first saw it.

I remember waking in the train early one morning, and looking out of the window at heavy forest trees of every description but mostly sal and shisharm; here and there a forest glade, or a stream of clear water—quite different from the muddied waters of the streams and rivers we had crossed the previous day. As we passed over a largish river (the Song) we saw a herd of elephants bathing; and leaving the forests of the Siwalik hills, we entered the Doon valley, where fields of rice and flowering mustard stretched away to the foothills.

Outside the station we climbed into a tonga, or pony trap, and rolled creakingly along quiet roads until we reached my grandmother's house. Grandfather had died a couple of years previously and Grandmother lived alone, except for occasional visits from her married daughters and their families, and from her unmarred but wandering son Ken, who was to turn up from time to time, especially when his funds were low. Granny also had a tenant, Miss Kellner, who occupied a portion of the bungalow.

Miss Kellner had been crippled in a carriage accident in Calcutta when she was a girl, and had ben confined to a chair all her adult life. She had been left some money by her parents, and was able to afford an ayah and four stout palanquin-bearers, who carried her about when she wanted the chair moved, and took her for outings in a real sedan chair or sometimes a rickshaw—she had both. Her hands were deformed and she could scarcely hold a pen, but she managed to play cards quite dexterously and taught me a number of card games, which I have now forgotten. Miss Kellner was the only person with whom I could play cards: she allowed me to cheat.

Granny employed a full-time gardener, a wizened old character named Dhuki (Sad), and I don't remember that he ever laughed or smiled. I'm not sure what deep tragedy dwelt behind those dark eyes (he never spoke about himself, even when questioned) but he was tolerant of me, and talked to me about the flowers and their characteristics.

There were rows and rows of sweet peas; beds full of phlox and sweet-smelling snapdragons; geraniums on the verandah steps, hollyhocks along the garden wall. Behind the house were the fruit trees, somewhat neglected since my grandfather's death, and it was here that I liked to wander in the afternoons, for the old orchard was dark and private and full of possibilities. I made friends with an old jackfruit tree, in whose trunk was a large hole in which I stored marbles, coins, catapults, and other treasures, much as a crow stores the bright objects it picks up during its peregrinations.

I have never been a great tree-climber, having a tendency to fall off branches, but I liked climbing walls (and still do), and it was not long before I had climbed the wall behind the orchard, to drop into unknown territory and explore the bazaars and by-lanes of Dehra.

# Who Kissed Me in the Dark?

This chapter, or story, could not have been written but for a phone call I received last week. I'll come to the caller later. Suffice to say that it triggered off memories of a hilarious fortnight in the autumn of that year (can't remember which one) when India and Pakistan went to war with each other. It did not last long, but there was plenty of excitement in our small town, set off by a rumour that enemy parachutists were landing in force in the ravine below Pari Tibba.

The road to this ravine led past my dwelling, and one afternoon I was amazed to see the town's constabulary, followed by hundreds of concerned citizens (armed mostly with hockey sticks) taking the trail down to the little stream where I usually went bird-watching. The parachutes turned out to be bedsheets from a nearby school, spread out to dry by the dhobis who lived on the opposite hill. After days of incessant rain the sun had come out, and the dhobis had finally got a chance to dry the school bedsheets on the verdant hillside. From afar they did look a bit like open parachutes. In times of crisis, it's wonderful what the imagination will do.

There were also black-outs. It's hard for a hill station to black itself out, but we did our best. Two or three respectable people were arrested for using their torches to find their way home in the dark. And of course, nothing could be done about the lights on the next mountain, as the people there did not even know there was a war on. They did not have radio or television or even electricity. They used kerosene lamps or lit bonfires!

We had a smart young set in Mussoorie in those days, mostly college students who had also been to convent schools and some of them decided it would be a good idea to put on a show—or old-fashioned theatrical extravaganza—to raise funds for the war effort. And they thought it would be a good idea to rope me in, as I was the only writer living in Mussoorie in those innocent times. I was thirty-one and I had never been a college student but they felt I was the right person to direct a one-act play in English. This was to be the centrepiece of the show.

I forget the name of the play. It was one of those drawing-room situation comedies popular from the 1920s, inspired by such successes as *Charley' Aunt* and *Tons of Money*. Anyway, we went into morning rehearsals at Hakman's, one of the older hotels, where there was a proper stage and a hall large enough to seat at least two hundred spectators.

The participants were full of enthusiasm, and rehearsals went along quite smoothly. They were an engaging bunch of young people—Guttoo, the intellectual among them; Ravi, a schoolteacher; Gita, a tiny ball of fire; Neena, a heavy-footed Bharatnatyam exponent; Nellie, daughter of a nurse; Chameli, who was in charge of make-up (she worked in a local beauty saloon); Rajiv, who served in the bar and was also our prompter; and a host of others, some of whom would sing and dance before and after our one-act play.

The performance was well attended, Ravi having rounded up a number of students from the local schools; and the lights were working, although we had to cover all doors, windows and exits with blankets to maintain the regulatory black-out. But the stage was old and rickety and things began to go wrong during Neena's dance number when, after a dazzling pirouette, she began stamping her feet and promptly went through the floorboards. Well, to be precise, her lower half went through, while the rest of her remained above board and visible to the audience.

The schoolboys cheered, the curtain came down and we rescued Neena, who had to be sent to the civil hospital with a sprained ankle, Mussoorie's only civilian war casualty.

There was a hold-up, but before the audience could get too restless the curtain went up on our play, a tea-party scene, which opened with Guttoo pouring tea for everyone. Unfortunately, our stage manager had forgotten to put any tea in the pot and poor Guttoo looked terribly put out as he went from cup to cup, pouring invisible tea. 'Damn. What happened to the tea?' muttered Guttoo, a line, which was not in the script. 'Never mind,' said Gita, playing opposite him and keeping her cool. 'I prefer my milk without tea,' and proceeded to pour herself a cup of milk.

After this, everyone began to fluff their lines and our prompter had a busy time. Unfortunately, he'd helped himself to a couple of rums at the bar, so that, whenever one of the actors faltered, he'd call out the correct words in a stentorian voice which could be heard all over the hall. Soon there was more prompting than acting and the audience began joining in with dialogue of their own.

Finally, to my great relief, the curtain came down—to thunderous applause. It went up again, and the cast stepped forward to take a bow. Our prompter, who was also the curtain-puller, released the ropes prematurely and the curtain came down with a rush, one of the sandbags hitting poor Guttoo on the head. He has never fully recovered from the blow.

The lights, which had been behaving all evening, now failed us, and we had a real black-out. In the midst of this confusion, someone—it must have been a girl, judging from the overpowering scent of jasmine that clung to her—put her arms around me and kissed me.

When the light came on again, she had vanished.

Who had kissed me in the dark?

As no one came forward to admit to the deed, I could only make wild guesses. But it had been a very sweet kiss, and I would have been only too happy to return it had I known its ownership. I could hardly go up to each of the girls and kiss them in the hope of reciprocation. After all, it might even have been someone from the audience.

Anyway, our concert did raise a few hundred rupees for the war effort. By the time we sent the money to the right authorities, the war was over. Hopefully they saw to it that the money was put to good use.

We went our various ways and although the kiss lingered in my mind, it gradually became a distant, fading memory and as the years passed it went out of my head altogether. Until the other day, almost forty years later...

'Phone for you,' announced Gautam, my seven-year-old secretary.

'Boy or girl? Man or woman?'

'Don't know. Deep voice like my teacher but it says you know her.'

'Ask her name.'

Gautam asked.

'She's Nellie, and she's speaking from Bareilly.'

'Nellie from Bareilly?' I was intrigued. I took the phone. 'Hello,' I said. 'I'm Bonda from Golconda.'

'Then you must be wealthy now.' Her voice was certainly husky. 'But don't you remember me? Nellie? I acted in that play of yours, up in Mussoorie a long time ago.'

'Of course, I remember now,' I was remembering. 'You had a small part, the maidservant I think. You were very pretty. You had dark, sultry eyes. But what made you ring me after all these years?'

'Well, I was thinking of you. I've often thought about you. You were much older than me, but I liked you. After that show, when the lights went out, I came up to you and kissed you. And then I ran away.'

'So it was you! I've often wondered. But why did you run away? I would have returned the kiss. More than once.'

'I was very nervous. I thought you'd be angry.'

'Well, I suppose it's too late now. You must be happily married with lots of children.'

'Husband left me. Children grew up, went away.'

'It must be lonely for you.'

'I have lots of dogs.'

'How many?'

'About thirty.'

'Thirty dogs! Do you run a kennel club?'

'No, they are all strays. I run a dog shelter.'

'Well, that's very good of you. Very humane.'

'You must come and see it sometime. Come to Bareilly. Stay with me. You like dogs, don't you?'

'Er-yes, of course. Man's best friend, the dog. But thirty is a lot of dogs to have about the house.'

'I have lots of space.'

'I'm sure... well, Nellie, if ever I'm in Bareilly, I'll come to see you. And I'm glad you phoned and cleared up the mystery. It was a lovely kiss and I'll always remember it.'

We said our goodbyes and I promised to visit her some day. A trip to Bareilly to return a kiss might seem a bit far-fetched, but I've done sillier things in my life. It's those dogs that worry me. I can imagine them snapping at my heels as I attempt to approach their mistress. Dogs can be very possessive.

'Who was that on the phone?' asked Gautam, breaking in on my reverie.

'Just an old friend!'

'Dada's old girlfriend. Are you going to see her?'

'I'll think about it.'

And I'm still thinking about it and about those dogs. But bliss it was to be in Mussoorie forty years ago, when Nellie kissed me in the dark.

Some memories are best left untouched.

# From Small Beginnings

*And the last puff of the day-wind brought from the unseen villages the scent of damp wood-smoke, hot cakes, dripping undergrowth, and rotting pine-cones. That is the true smell of the Himalayas, and if once it creeps into the blood of a man, that man will at the last, forgetting all else, return to the hills to die.*

—Rudyard Kipling

On the first clear September day, towards the end of the rains, I visited the pine knoll, my place of peace and power. It was months since I'd last been there. Trips to the plains, a crisis in my affairs, involvements with other people and their troubles, and an entire monsoon had come between me and the grassy, pine-topped slope facing the Hill of Fairies (Pari Tibba to the locals). Now I tramped through late monsoon foliage—tall ferns, bushes festooned with flowering convolvulus—and crossed the stream by way of its little bridge of stones before climbing the steep hill to the pine slope.

When the trees saw me, they made as if to turn in my direction. A puff of wind came across the valley from the distant snows. A long-tailed blue magpie took alarm and flew noisily out of an oak tree. The cicadas were suddenly silent. But the trees remembered me. They bowed gently in the breeze and beckoned me nearer, welcoming me home. Three pines, a straggling oak and a wild cherry. I went among them and acknowledged their welcome with a touch of my hand against their trunks—the cherry's smooth and polished; the pine's patterned and whorled; the oak's rough, gnarled, full of experience. He'd been there longest, and the wind had bent his upper branches and twisted a few, so that he looked shaggy and undistinguished. But like the philosopher who is careless about his dress and appearance, the oak has secrets, a hidden wisdom. He has learnt the art of survival!

While the oak and the pines are older than me and have been here many years, the cherry tree is exactly seven years old. I know, because I planted it.

One day I had this cherry seed in my hand, and on an impulse I thrust it into the soft earth, and then went away and forgot all about it. A few months later I found a tiny cherry tree in the long grass. I did not expect it to survive. But the following year it was two feet tall. And then some goats ate its leaves and a grass cutter's scythe injured the stem, and I was sure it would wither away. But it renewed itself, sprang up even faster, and within three years it was a healthy, growing tree, about five feet tall.

I left the hills for two years—forced by circumstances to make a living in Delhi—but this time I did not forget the cherry tree. I thought about it fairly often, sent telepathic messages of encouragement in its direction. And when, a couple of years ago, I returned in the autumn, my heart did a somersault when I found my tree sprinkled with pale pink blossom (the Himalayan cherry flowers in November). And later, when the fruit was ripe, the tree was visited by finches, tits, bulbuls and other small birds, all come to feast on the sour, red cherries.

Last summer I spent a night on the pine knoll, sleeping on the grass beneath the cherry tree. I lay awake for hours, listening to the chatter of the stream and the occasional tonk-tonk of nightjars, and watching through the branches overhead, the stars turning in the sky. And I felt the power of the sky and the earth, and the power of a small cherry seed...

And so when the rains are over, this is where I come, that I might feel the peace and power of this place.

This is where I will write my stories. I can see everything from here—my cottage across the valley; behind and above me, the town and the bazaar, straddling the ridge; to the left, the high mountains and the twisting road to the source of the great river; below me, the little stream and the path to the village; ahead, the Hill of Fairies and the fields beyond; the wide valley below, and another range of hills and then the distant plains. I can even see Prem Singh in the garden, putting the mattresses out in the sun.

From here he is just a speck on the far hill, but I know it is Prem by the way he stands. A man may have a hundred disguises, but in the end it is his posture that gives him away. Like my grandfather, who was a master of disguise and successfully roamed the bazaars as fruit vendor or basket maker. But we could always recognize him because of his pronounced slouch.

Prem Singh doesn't slouch, but he has this habit of looking up at the sky (regardless of whether it's cloudy or clear), and at the moment he's looking at the sky.

Eight years with Prem. He was just a sixteen-year-old boy when I first saw him, and now he has a wife and child.

I had been in the cottage for just over a year... He stood on the landing outside the kitchen door. A tall boy, dark, with good teeth and brown, deep-set eyes, dressed smartly in white drill—his only change of clothes. Looking for a job. I liked the look of him, but—

'I already have someone working for me,' I said.

'Yes, sir. He is my uncle.'

In the hills, everyone is a brother or an uncle.

'You don't want me to dismiss your uncle?'

'No, sir. But he says you can find a job for me.'

'I'll try. I'll make inquiries. Have you just come from your village?'

'Yes. Yesterday I walked ten miles to Pauri. There I got a bus.'

'Sit down. Your uncle will make some tea.'

He sat down on the steps, removed his white keds, wriggled his toes. His feet were both long and broad, large feet but not ugly. He was unusually clean for a hill boy. And taller than most.

'Do you smoke?' I asked.

'No, sir.'

'It is true,' said his uncle. 'He does not smoke. All my nephews smoke, but this one. He is a little peculiar, he does not smoke—neither beedi nor hookah.'

'Do you drink?'

'It makes me vomit.'

'Do you take bhang?'

'No, sahib.'

'You have no vices. It's unnatural.'

'He is unnatural, sahib,' said his uncle.

'Does he chase girls?'

'They chase him, sahib.'

'So he left the village and came looking for a job.' I looked at him. He grinned, then looked away and began rubbing his feet.

'Your name is...?'

'Prem Singh.'

'All right, Prem, I will try to do something for you.'

I did not see him for a couple of weeks. I forgot about finding him a job. But when I met him again, on the road to the bazaar, he told me that he had got a temporary job in the Survey, looking after the surveyor's tents.

'Next week we will be going to Rajasthan,' he said.

'It will be very hot. Have you been in the desert before?'

'No, sir.'

'It is not like the hills. And it is far from home.'

'I know. But I have no choice in the matter. I have to collect some money in order to get married.'

In his region there was a bride price, usually of 2,000 rupees.

'Do you have to get married so soon?'

'I have only one brother and he is still very young. My mother is not well. She needs a daughter-in-law to help her in the fields and with the cows and in the house. We are a small family, so the work is greater.'

Every family has its few terraced fields, narrow and stony,

usually perched on a hillside above a stream or river. They grow rice, barley, maize, potatoes—just enough to live on. Even if their produce is sufficient for marketing, the absence of roads makes it difficult to get the produce to the market towns. There is no money to be earned in the villages, and money is needed for clothes, soap, medicines, and for recovering the family jewellery from the moneylenders. So the young men leave their villages to find work, and to find work they must go to the plains. The lucky ones get into the army. Others enter domestic service or take jobs in garages, hotels, wayside tea shops, schools...

In Mussoorie, the main attraction is the large number of schools which employ cooks and bearers. But the schools were full when Prem arrived. He'd been to the recruiting centre at Roorkee, hoping to get into the army; but they found a deformity in his right foot, the result of a bone broken when a landslip carried him away one dark monsoon night. He was lucky, he said, that it was only his foot and not his head that had been broken.

He came to the house to inform his uncle about the job and to say goodbye. I thought, another nice person I probably won't see again; another ship passing in the night, the friendly twinkle of its lights soon vanishing in the darkness. I said 'come again,' held his smile with mine so that I could remember him better, and returned to my study and my typewriter. The typewriter is the repository of a writer's loneliness. It stares unsympathetically back at him every day, doing its best to be discouraging. Maybe I'll go back to the old-fashioned quill pen and marble inkstand; then I can feel like a real writer—Balzac or Dickens—scratching away into the endless reaches of the night... Of course, the days and nights are seemingly shorter than they need to be! They must be, otherwise why do we hurry so much and achieve so little, by the standards of the past...

Prem goes, disappears into the vast faceless cities of the plains, and a year slips by, or rather I do, and then here he is again, thinner and darker, and still smiling and looking for a job. I should have known that hillmen don't disappear altogether. The spirit-haunted rocks don't let their people wander too far, lest they lose them forever.

I was able to get him a job in the school. The headmaster's wife needed a cook. I wasn't sure if Prem could cook very well but I sent him along and they said they'd give him a trial. Three days later the headmaster's wife met me on the road and started gushing all over me. She was the type who gushed.

'We're so grateful to you! Thank you for sending me that lovely boy. He's so polite. And he cooks very well. A little too hot for my husband, but otherwise delicious—just delicious! He's a real treasure—a lovely boy.' And she gave me an arch look—the famous look which she used to captivate all the good looking young prefects who became prefects, it was said, only if she approved of them.

I wasn't sure that she didn't want something more than a cook, and I only hoped that Prem would give every satisfaction.

He looked cheerful enough when he came to see me on his off day.

'How are you getting on?' I asked.

'Lovely,' he said, using his mistress's favourite expression.

'What do you mean—lovely? Do they like your work?'

'The memsahib likes it. She strokes me on the cheek

whenever she enters the kitchen. The sahib says nothing. He takes medicine after every meal.'

'Did he always take medicine—or only now that you're doing the cooking?'

'I am not sure. I think he has always been sick.'

He was sleeping in the headmaster's verandah and getting sixty rupees a month. A cook in Delhi got a hundred and sixty. And a cook in Paris or New York got ten times as much. I did not say as much to Prem. He might ask me to get him a job in New York. And that would be the last I saw of him! He, as a cook, might well get a job making curries off-Broadway; I, as a writer, wouldn't get to first base. And only my Uncle Ken knew the secret of how to make a living without actually doing any work. But then, of course, he had four sisters. And each of them was married to a fairly prosperous husband. So Uncle Ken divided his year among them. Three months with Aunt Ruby in Nainital. Three months with Aunt Susie in Kashmir. Three months with my mother (not quite so affluent) in Jamnagar. And three months in the Vet Hospital in Bareilly, where Aunt Mabel ran the hospital for her veterinary husband. In this way, he never overstayed his welcome. A sister can look after a brother for just three months at a time and no more. Uncle K had it worked out to perfection.

But I had no sisters and I couldn't live forever on the royalties of a single novel. So I had to write others. So I came to the hills.

The hillmen go to the plains to make a living. I had to come to the hills to try and make mine.

'Prem,' I said, 'why don't you work for me?'

'And what about my uncle?'

'He seems ready to desert me any day. His grandfather is ill, he says, and he wants to go home.'

'His grandfather died last year.'

'That's what I mean—he's getting restless. And I don't mind if he goes. These days he seems to be suffering from a form of sleeping sickness. I have to get up first and make his tea...'

Sitting here under the cherry tree, whose leaves are just beginning to turn yellow, I rest my chin on my knees and gaze across the valley to where Prem moves about in the garden. Looking back over the seven years he has been with me, I recall some of the nicest things about him. They come to me in no particular order—just pieces of cinema—coloured slides slipping across the screen of memory...

Prem rocking his infant son to sleep—crooning to him, passing his large hand gently over the child's curly head—Prem following me down to the police station when I was arrested (on a warrant from Bombay, charging me with writing an allegedly obscene short story!), and waiting outside until I reappeared— his smile, when I found him in Delhi, his large, irrepressible laughter, most in evidence when he was seeing an old Laurel and Hardy movie.

Of course, there were times when he could be infuriating, stubborn, deliberately pig-headed, sending me little notes of resignation—but I never found it difficult to overlook these little acts of self-indulgence. He had brought much love and laughter into my life, and what more could a lonely man ask for?

It was his stubborn streak that limited the length of his stay in the headmaster's household. Mr Good was tolerant enough. But Mrs Good was one of those women who, when they are pleased with you, go out of their way to help, pamper and flatter, but when displeased, become vindictive, going out of their way to harm or destroy. Mrs Good sought power—over her husband, her dog, her favourite pupils, her servant... She had absolute power over the husband and the dog, partial power over her slightly bewildered pupils, and none at all over Prem, who missed the subtleties of her designs upon his soul. He did not respond to her mothering, or to the way in which she tweaked him on the cheeks, brushed against him in the kitchen and made admiring remarks about his looks and physique. Memsahibs, he knew, were not for him. So he kept a stony face and went diligently about his duties. And she felt slighted, put in her place. Her liking turned to dislike. Instead of admiring remarks, she began making disparaging remarks about his looks, his clothes, his manners. She found fault with his cooking. No longer was it 'lovely'. She even accused him of taking away the dog's meat and giving it to a poor family living on the hillside—no more heinous crime could be imagined! Mr Good threatened him with dismissal. So Prem became stubborn. The following day he withheld the dog's food altogether, threw it down the khud where it was seized upon by innumerable strays, and went off to the pictures.

That was the end of his job. 'I'll have to go home now,' he told me. 'I won't get another job in this area. The mem will see to that.'

'Stay a few days,' I said.

'I have only enough money with which to get home.'

'Keep it for going home. You can stay with me for a few days, while you look around. Your uncle won't mind sharing his food with you.'

His uncle did mind. He did not like the idea of working for his nephew as well; it seemed to him no part of his duties. And he was apprehensive that Prem might get his job.

So Prem stayed no longer than a week.

Here on the knoll the grass is just beginning to turn October yellow. The first clouds approaching winter cover the sky. The trees are very still. The birds are silent. Only a cricket keeps singing on the oak tree. Perhaps there will be a storm before evening. A storm like the one in which Prem arrived at the cottage with his wife and child—but that's jumping too far ahead...

After he had returned to his village, it was several months before I saw him again. His uncle told me he had taken up a job in Delhi. There was an address. It did not seem complete, but I resolved that when I was next in Delhi I would try to see him.

The opportunity came in May, as the hot winds of summer blew across the plains. It was the time of year when people who can afford it, try to get away to the hills. I dislike New Delhi at the best of times, and I hate it in summer. People compete with each other in being bad-tempered and mean. But I had to go down—I don't remember why, but it must have seemed very necessary at the time—and I took the opportunity to try and see Prem.

Nothing went right for me. Of course the address was all wrong, and I wandered about in a remote, dusty, treeless colony called Vasant Vihar (Spring Garden) for over two hours, asking all the domestic servants I came across if they could put me in touch with Prem Singh of Village Koli, Pauri Garhwal.

There were innumerable Prem Singhs, but apparently none who belonged to Village Koli. I returned to my hotel and took two days to recover from heatstroke before returning to Mussoorie, thanking God for mountains!

And then the uncle gave notice. He'd found a better-paid job in Dehra Dun and was anxious to be off. I didn't try to stop him.

For the next six months, I lived in the cottage without any help. I did not find this difficult. I was used to living alone. It wasn't service that I needed but companionship. In the cottage it was very quiet. The ghosts of long-dead residents were sympathetic but unobtrusive. The song of the whistling thrush was beautiful, but I knew he was not singing for me. Up the valley came the sound of a flute, but I never saw the flute player. My affinity was with the little red fox who roamed the hillside below the cottage. I met him one night and wrote these lines:

As I walked home last night
I saw a lone fox dancing
In the cold moonlight.
I stood and watched—then
Took the low road, knowing
the night was his by right.
Sometimes, when words ring true,
I'm like a lone fox dancing
In the morning dew.

During the rains, watching the dripping trees and the mist climbing the valley, I wrote a great deal of poetry. Loneliness is of value to poets. But poetry didn't bring me much money, and funds were low. And then, just as I was wondering if I would have to give up my freedom and take a job again, a publisher bought the paperback rights of one of my children's stories, and I was free to live and write as I pleased—for another three months!

That was in November. To celebrate, I took a long walk through the Landour bazaar and up the Tehri road. It was a good day for walking; and it was dark by the time I returned to the outskirts of the town. Someone stood waiting for me on the road above the cottage. I hurried past him.

If I am not for myself,
Who will be for me?
And if I am not for others,
What am I?
And if not now, when?

I startled myself with the memory of these words of Hillel, the ancient Hebrew sage. I walked back to the shadows where the youth stood, and saw that it was Prem.

'Prem!' I said. 'Why are you sitting out here, in the cold? Why did you not go to the house?'

'I went, sir, but there was a lock on the door. I thought you had gone away.'

'And you were going to remain here, on the road?'

'Only for tonight. I would have gone down to Dehra in the morning.'

'Come, let's go home. I have been waiting for you. I looked for you in Delhi, but could not find the place where you were working.'

'I have left them now.'

'And your uncle has left me. So will you work for me now?'

'For as long as you wish.'

'For as long as the gods wish.'

We did not go straight home, but returned to the bazaar and took our meal in the Sindhi Sweet Shop—hot puris and strong sweet tea.

We walked home together in the bright moonlight. I felt sorry for the little fox dancing alone.

That was twenty years ago, and Prem and his wife and three children are still with me. But we live in a different house now, on another hill.

# The Girl on the Train

I had the train compartment to myself up to Rohana, then a girl got in. The couple who saw her off were probably her parents; they seemed very anxious about her comfort, and the woman gave the girl detailed instructions as to where to keep her things, when not to lean out of windows, and how to avoid speaking to strangers.

They called their goodbyes and the train pulled out of the station. As I was going blind at the time, my eyes sensitive only to light and darkness, I was unable to tell what the girl looked like; but I knew she wore slippers from the way they slapped against her heels.

It would take me some time to discover something about her looks, and perhaps I never would. But I liked the sound of her voice, and even the sound of her slippers.

'Are you going all the way to Dehra?' I asked.

I must have been sitting in a dark corner, because my voice startled her. She gave a little exclamation and said, 'I didn't know anyone else was here.'

Well, it often happens that people with good eyesight fail to see what is right in front of them. They have too much to take in, I suppose. Whereas people who cannot see (or see very little) have to take in only the essentials, whatever registers most tellingly on their remaining senses.

'I didn't see you either,' I said. 'But I heard you come in.'

I wondered if I would be able to prevent her from discovering that I was blind. Provided I keep to my seat, I thought, it shouldn't be too difficult.

The girl said, 'I'm getting off at Saharanpur. My aunt is meeting me there.'

'Then I had better not get too familiar,' I replied. 'Aunts are usually formidable creatures.'

'Where are you going?' she asked.

'To Dehra, and then to Mussoorie.'

'Oh, how lucky you are. I wish I were going to Mussoorie. I love the hills. Especially in October.'

'Yes, this is the best time,' I said, calling on my memories. 'The hills are covered with wild dahlias, the sun is delicious, and at night you can sit in front of a logfire and drink a little brandy. Most of the tourists have gone, and the roads are quiet and almost deserted. Yes, October is the best time.'

She was silent. I wondered if my words had touched her, or whether she thought me a romantic fool. Then I made a mistake.

'What is it like outside?' I asked.

She seemed to find nothing strange in the question. Had she noticed already that I could not see? But her next question removed my doubts.

'Why don't you look out of the window?' she asked.

I moved easily along the berth and felt for the window ledge. The window was open, and I faced it, making a pretence of studying the landscape. I heard the panting of the engine, the rumble of the wheels, and, in my mind's eye, I could see telegraph posts flashing by.

'Have you noticed,' I ventured, 'that the trees seem to be moving while we seem to be standing still?'

'That always happens,' she said. 'Do you see any animals?'

'No,' I answered quite confidently. I knew that there were hardly any animals left in the forests near Dehra.

I turned from the window and faced the girl, and for a while we sat in silence.

'You have an interesting face,' I remarked. I was becoming quite daring, but it was a safe remark. Few girls can resist flattery. She laughed pleasantly—a clear ringing laugh.

'It's nice to be told I have an interesting face. I'm tired of people telling me I have a pretty face.'

Oh, so you do have a pretty face, thought I; and aloud I said, 'Well, an interesting face can also be pretty.'

'You are a very gallant young man,' she said 'but why are you so serious?'

I thought, then, I would try to laugh for her, but the thought of laughter only made me feel troubled and lonely.

'We'll soon be at your station,' I said.

'Thank goodness it's a short journey. I can't bear to sit in a train for more than two or three hours.'

Yet I was prepared to sit there for almost any length of time, just to listen to her talking. Her voice had the sparkle of a mountain stream. As soon as she left the train, she would forget our brief encounter; but it would stay with me for the rest of the journey, and for some time after.

The engine's whistle shrieked, the carriage wheels changed their sound and rhythm, the girl got up and began to collect her things. I wondered if she wore her hair in a bun, or if it was plaited; perhaps it was hanging loose over her shoulders, or was it cut very short?

The train drew slowly into the station. Outside, there was the shouting of porters and vendors and a high-pitched female voice near the carriage door; that voice must have belonged to the girl's aunt.

'Goodbye,' the girl said.

She was standing very close to me, so close that the perfume from her hair was tantalizing. I wanted to raise my hand and touch her hair, but she moved away. Only the scent of perfume still lingered where she had stood.

There was some confusion in the doorway. A man, getting into the compartment, stammered an apology. Then the door banged, and the world was shut out again. I returned to my berth. The guard blew his whistle and we moved off. Once again, I had a game to play and a new fellow traveller.

The train gathered speed, the wheels took up their song, the carriage groaned and shook. I found the window and sat in front of it, staring into the daylight that was darkness for me.

So many things were happening outside the window: it could be a fascinating game, guessing what went on out there.

The man who had entered the compartment broke into my reverie.

'You must be disappointed,' he said. 'I'm not nearly as attractive a travelling companion as the one who just left.'

'She was an interesting girl,' I said. 'Can you tell me—did she keep her hair long or short?'

'I don't remember,' he said, sounding puzzled. 'It was her eyes I noticed, not her hair. She had beautiful eyes—but they were of no use to her. She was completely blind. Didn't you notice?'

# Sounds I Like to Hear

All night the rain has been drumming on the corrugated tin roof. There has been no storm, no thunder, just the steady swish of a tropical downpour. It helps one to lie awake; at the same time, it doesn't keep one from sleeping.

It is a good sound to read by—the rain outside, the quiet within—and, although tin roofs are given to springing unaccountable leaks, there is in general a feeling of being untouched by, and yet in touch with, the rain.

Gentle rain on a tin roof is one of my favourite sounds. And early in the morning, when the rain has stopped, there are other sounds I like to hear—a crow shaking the raindrops from his feathers and cawing rather disconsolately; babblers and bulbuls bustling in and out of bushes and long grass in search of worms and insects; the sweet, ascending trill of the Himalayan whistling thrush; dogs rushing through damp undergrowth.

A cherry tree, bowed down by the heavy rain, suddenly rights itself, flinging pellets of water in my face.

Some of the best sounds are made by water. The water of

a mountain stream, always in a hurry, bubbling over rocks and chattering, 'I'm late, I'm late!' like the White Rabbit, tumbling over itself in its anxiety to reach the bottom of the hill, the sound of the sea, especially when it is far away—or when you hear it by putting a seashell to your ear. The sound made by dry and thirsty earth, as it sucks at a sprinkling of water. Or the sound of a child drinking thirstily, the water running down his chin and throat.

Water gushing out of the pans of an old well outside a village while a camel moves silently round the well. Bullock cart wheels creaking over rough country roads. The clip clop of a pony carriage, and the tinkle of its bell, and the sing-song call of its driver...

Bells in the hills. A school bell ringing, and children's voices drifting through an open window. A temple bell, heard faintly from across the valley. Heavy silver ankle bells on the feet of sturdy hill women. Sheep bells heard high up on the mountainside.

Do falling petals make a sound? Just the tiniest and softest of sounds, like the drift of falling snow. Of course big flowers, like dahlias, drop their petals with a very definite flop. These are show-offs, like the hawk moth who comes flapping into the rooms at night instead of emulating the butterfly dipping lazily on the afternoon breeze.

One must return to the birds for favourite sounds, and the birds of the plains differ from the birds of the hills. On a cold winter morning in the plains of northern India, if you walk some way into the jungle you will hear the familiar call of the black partridge: *'Bhagwan teri qudrat'* it seems to cry, which means: 'Oh God! Great is thy might.'

The cry rises from the bushes in all directions; but an hour later not a bird is to be seen or heard and the jungle is so very still that the silence seems to shout at you.

There are sounds that come from a distance, beautiful because they are far away, voices on the wind—they 'walketh upon the wings of the wind'. The cries of fishermen out on the river. Drums beating rhythmically in a distant village. The croaking of frogs from the rainwater pond behind the house. I mean frogs at a distance. A frog croaking beneath one's window is as welcome as a motor horn.

But some people like motor horns. I know a taxi driver who never misses an opportunity to use his horn. It was made to his own specifications, and it gives out a resonant bugle call. He never tires of using it. Cyclists and pedestrians always scatter at his approach. Other cars veer off the road. He is proud of his horn. He loves its strident sound—which only goes to show that some men's sounds are other men's noises!

Homely sounds, though we don't often think about them, are the ones we miss most when they are gone. A kettle on the boil. A door that creaks on its hinges. Old sofa springs. Familiar voices lighting up the dark. Ducks quacking in the rain.

And so we return to the rain, with which my favourite sounds began.

I have sat out in the open at night, after a shower of rain when the whole air is murmuring and tinkling with the voices of crickets and grasshoppers and little frogs. There is one melodious sound, a sweet repeated trill, which I have never been able to trace to its source. Perhaps it is a little tree frog. Or it may be a small green cricket. I shall never know.

I am not sure that I really want to know. In an age when a scientific and rational explanation has been given for almost everything we see and touch and hear, it is good to be left with one small mystery, a mystery sweet and satisfying and entirely my own.

## Listen!

Listen to the night wind in the trees,
Listen to the summer grass singing;
Listen to the time that's tripping by,
And the dawn dew falling.
Listen to the moon as it climbs the sky,
Listen to the pebbles humming;
Listen to the mist in the trembling leaves,
And the silence calling.

# The Monkeys

I couldn't be sure, next morning, if I had been dreaming or if I had really heard dogs barking in the night and had seen them scampering about on the hillside below the cottage. There had been a golden Cocker, a Retriever, a Peke, a Dachshund, a black Labrador and one or two nondescripts. They had woken me with their barking shortly after midnight, and had made so much noise that I had got out of bed and looked out of the open window. I saw them quite plainly in the moonlight, five or six dogs rushing excitedly through the bracket and long monsoon grass.

It was only because there had been so many breeds among the dogs that I felt a little confused. I had been in the cottage only a week, and I was already on nodding or speaking terms with most of my neighbours. Colonel Fanshawe, retired from the Indian army, was my immediate neighbour. He did keep a Cocker, but it was black. The elderly Anglo-Indian spinsters who lived beyond the deodars kept only cats. (Though why cats should be the prerogative of spinsters, I have never been able to understand.) The milkman kept a couple of mongrels. And the Punjabi industrialist who had bought a former prince's palace—without ever occupying it—left the property in charge of a watchman who kept a huge Tibetan mastiff.

None of these dogs looked like the ones I had seen in the night.

'Does anyone here keep a Retriever?' I asked Colonel Fanshawe, when I met him taking his evening walk.

'No one that I know of,' he said and gave me a swift, penetrating look from under his bushy eyebrows. 'Why, have you seen one around?'

'No, I just wondered. There are a lot of dogs in the area, aren't there?'

'Oh, yes. Nearly everyone keeps a dog here. Of course, every now and then a panther carries one off. Lost a lovely little terrier myself only last winter.'

Colonel Fanshawe, tall and red-faced, seemed to be waiting for me to tell him something more—or was he just taking time to recover his breath after a stiff uphill climb?

That night I heard the dogs again. I went to the window and looked out. The moon was at the full, silvering the leaves of the oak trees.

The dogs were looking up into the trees and barking. But I could see nothing in the trees, not even an owl.

I gave a shout, and the dogs disappeared into the forest.

Colonel Fanshawe looked at me expectantly when I met him the following day. He knew something about those dogs, of that I was certain; but he was waiting to hear what I had to say. I decided to oblige him.

'I saw at least six dogs in the middle of the night,' I said. 'A Cocker, a Retriever, a Peke, a Dachshund and two mongrels. Now, Colonel, I'm sure you must know whose they are.'

The Colonel was delighted. I could tell by the way his eyes glinted that he was going to enjoy himself at my expense. 'You've been seeing Miss Fairchild's dogs,' he said with smug satisfaction.

'Oh, and where does she live?'

'She doesn't, my boy. Died fifteen years ago.'

'Then what are her dogs doing here?'

'Looking for monkeys,' said the Colonel. And he stood back to watch my reaction.

'I'm afraid I don't understand,' I said.

'Let me put it this way,' said the Colonel. 'Do you believe in ghosts?'

'I've never seen any,' I said.

'But you have, my boy, you have. Miss Fairchild's dogs died years ago—a Cocker, a Retriever, a Dachshund, a Peke and two mongrels. They were buried on a little knoll under the oaks. Nothing odd about their deaths, mind you. They were all quite old, and didn't survive their mistress very long. Neighbours looked after them until they died.'

'And Miss Fairchild lived in the cottage where I stay? Was she young?'

'She was in her mid-forties, an athletic sort of woman, fond of the outdoors. Didn't care much for men. I thought you knew about her.'

'No, I haven't been here very long, you know. But what was it you said about monkeys? Why were the dogs looking for monkeys?'

'Ah, that's the interesting part of the story. Have you seen the langoor monkeys that sometimes come to eat oak leaves?'

'No.'

'You will, sooner or later. There has always been a band of them roaming these forests. They're quite harmless really, except that they'll ruin a garden if given half a chance...Well, Miss Fairchild fairly loathed those monkeys. She was very keen on her dahlias—grew some prize specimens—but the monkeys would come at night, dig up the plants and eat the dahlia bulbs. Apparently they found the bulbs much to their liking. Miss Fairchild would be furious. People who are passionately fond of gardening often go off balance when their best plants are ruined—that's only human, I suppose. Miss Fairchild set her dogs on the monkeys whenever she could, even if it was in the middle of the night. But the monkeys simply took to the trees and left the dogs barking.

'Then one day—or rather one night—Miss Fairchild took desperate measures. She borrowed a shotgun and sat up near a window. And when the monkeys arrived, she shot one of them dead.'

The Colonel paused and looked out over the oak trees which were shimmering in the warm afternoon sun.

'She shouldn't have done that,' he said.

'Never shoot a monkey. It's not only that they're sacred to Hindus—but they are rather human, you know. Well, I must be getting on. Good day!' And the Colonel, having ended his story rather abruptly, set off at a brisk pace through the deodars.

I didn't hear the dogs that night. But the next day I saw the monkeys—the real ones, not ghosts. There were about twenty of them, young and old, sitting in the trees munching oak leaves. They didn't pay much attention to me, and I watched them for some time.

They were handsome creatures, their fur a silver-grey, their tails long and sinuous. They leapt gracefully from tree to tree, and were very polite and dignified in their behaviour towards each other—unlike the bold, rather crude red monkeys of the plains. Some of the younger ones scampered about on the hillside, playing and wrestling with each other like schoolboys.

There were no dogs to molest them—and no dahlias to tempt them into the garden.

But that night, I heard the dogs again. They were barking more furiously than ever.

'Well, I'm not getting up for them this time,' I mumbled, and pulled the blanket over my ears.

But the barking grew louder, and was joined by other sounds, a squealing and a scuffling.

Then suddenly, the piercing shriek of a woman rang through the forest. It was an unearthly sound, and it made my hair stand up.

I leapt out of bed and dashed to the window.

A woman was lying on the ground, three or four huge monkeys were on top of her, biting her arms and pulling at her throat. The dogs were yelping and trying to drag the monkeys off, but they were being harried from behind by others. The woman gave another bloodcurdling shriek, and I dashed back into the room, grabbed hold of a small axe and ran into the garden.

But everyone—dogs, monkeys and shrieking woman—had disappeared, and I stood alone on the hillside in my pyjamas, clutching an axe and feeling very foolish.

The Colonel greeted me effusively the following day.

'Still seeing those dogs?' he asked in a bantering tone.

'I've seen the monkeys too,' I said.

'Oh, yes, they've come around again. But they're real enough, and quite harmless.'

'I know—but I saw them last night with the dogs.' 'Oh, did you really? That's strange, very strange.' The Colonel tried to avoid my eye, but I hadn't quite finished with him.

'Colonel,' I said. 'You never did get around to telling me how Miss Fairchild died.'

'Oh, didn't I? Must have slipped my memory. I'm getting old, don't remember people as well as I used to. But, of course, I remember about Miss Fairchild, poor lady. The monkeys killed her. Didn't you know? They simply tore her to pieces...'

His voice trailed of, and he looked thoughtfully at a caterpillar that was making its way up his walking stick.

'She shouldn't have shot one of them,' he said. 'Never shoot a monkey—they're rather human, you know...'

# In Grandfather's Garden

Though the house and grounds of our home in Dehra were Grandfather's domain—where he kept an odd assortment of pets—the magnificent old banyan tree was mine, chiefly because Grandfather, at the age of sixty-five, could no longer climb it. Grandmother used to tease him about this, and would speak of a certain Countess of Desmond, an Englishwoman who lived till the age of 117, and would have lived longer if she hadn't fallen while climbing an apple tree. The spreading branches of the banyan tree, which curved to the ground and took root again, forming a maze of arches, gave me endless pleasure. The tree was older than the house, older than Grandfather, as old as the town of Dehra, nestling in a valley at the foot of the Himalayas.

My first friend was a small grey squirrel. Arching his back and sniffing into the air, he seemed at first to resent my invasion of his privacy. But when he found that I did not arm myself with a catapult or air-gun, he became friendlier. And when I started leaving him pieces of cake and biscuit, he grew bolder, and finally became familiar enough to take food from my hands.

Before long, he was delving into my pockets and helping himself to whatever he could find. He was a very young squirrel, and his friends and relatives probably thought of him as headstrong and foolish for trusting a human.

In the spring, when the banyan tree was full of small red figs, birds of all kinds would flock into its branches, the red-bottomed bulbul, cheerful and greedy; gossiping rosy pastors; and parrots and crows, squabbling with each other all the time. During the fig season, the banyan tree was the noisiest place on the road.

Halfway up the tree I had built a small platform on which I would often spend the afternoons when it wasn't too hot. I could read there, propping myself up against the bole of the tree with the cushions taken from the drawing room. *Treasure Island*, *Huckleberry Finn*, the Mowgli stories, and detective novels made up my bag of very mixed reading.

When I didn't want to read, I could look down through the banyan leaves at the world below, at Grandmother hanging up or taking down the washing, at the cook quarrelling with a fruit vendor, or at Grandfather grumbling at the hardy Indian marigold, which insisted on springing up all over his very English garden. Usually nothing very exciting happened while I was in the banyan tree, but on one particular afternoon I had enough excitement to last me through the summer.

That was the time I saw a mongoose and a cobra fight to death in the garden, while I sat directly above them in the banyan tree.

It was an April afternoon. The warm breezes of approaching

summer had sent everyone, including Grandfather, indoors. I was feeling drowsy myself and was wondering if I should go to the pond behind the house for a swim, when I saw a huge black cobra gliding out of a clump of cacti and making for some cooler part of the garden. At the same time a mongoose (whom I had often seen) emerged from the bushes and went straight for the cobra.

In a clearing beneath the tree, in bright sunshine, they came face to face.

The cobra knew only too well that the grey mongoose, three feet long, was a superb fighter, clever and aggressive. But the cobra was a skilful and experienced fighter, too. He could move swiftly and strike with the speed of light, and the sacs behind his long, sharp fangs were full of deadly venom.

It was to be a battle of champions.

Hissing defiance, his forked tongue darting in and out, the cobra raised three of his six feet off the ground, and spread his broad, spectacled hood. The mongoose bushed his tail. The long hair on his spine stood up (in the past, the very thickness of his hair had saved him from bites that would have been fatal to others).

Though the combatants were unaware of my presence in the banyan tree, they soon became aware of the arrival of two other spectators. One was a mynah and the other a jungle crow (not the wily urban crow). They had seen these preparations for battle, and had settled on the cactus to watch the outcome. Had they been content only to watch, all would have been well with both of them.

The cobra stood on the defensive, swaying slowly from side

to side, trying to mesmerize the mongoose into making a false move. The mongoose knew the power of his opponent's glassy, twinkling eyes, and refused to meet them. Instead, he fixed his gaze at a point just below the cobra's hood, and opened the attack.

Moving forward quickly until he was just within the cobra's reach, he made a feint to one side. Immediately, the cobra struck. His great hood came down so swiftly that I thought nothing could save the mongoose. But the little fellow jumped neatly to one side, and darted in as swiftly as the cobra, biting the snake on the back and darting away again out of reach.

The moment the cobra struck, the crow and the mynah hurled themselves at him, only to collide heavily in mid-air. Shrieking at each other, they returned to the cactus plant.

A few drops of blood glistened on the cobra's back.

The cobra struck again and missed. Again the mongoose sprang aside, jumped in and bit. Again the birds dived at the snake, bumped into each other instead, and returned shrieking to the safety of the cactus.

The third round followed the same course as the first but with one dramatic difference. The crow and the mynah, still determined to take part in the proceedings, dived at the cobra, but this time they missed each other as well as their mark. The mynah flew on and reached its perch, but the crow tried to pull up in mid-air and turn back. In the second that it took him to do this, the cobra whipped his head back and struck with great force, his snout thudding against the crow's body.

I saw the bird flung nearly twenty feet across the garden, where, after fluttering about for a while, it lay still. The mynah remained on the cactus plant, and when the snake and the mongoose returned to the fray, it very wisely refrained from interfering again!

The cobra was weakening, and the mongoose, walking fearlessly up to it, raised himself on his short legs, and with a lightning snap had the big snake by the snout. The cobra writhed and lashed about in a frightening manner, and even coiled itself about the mongoose, but all to no avail. The little fellow hung grimly on, until the snake had ceased to struggle. He then smeared along its quivering length, gripping it round the hood, and dragging it into the bushes.

The mynah dropped cautiously to the ground, hopped about, peered into the bushes from a safe distance, and then, with a shrill cry of congratulation, flew away.

When I had also made a cautious descent from the tree and returned to the house, I told Grandfather of the fight I had seen. He was pleased that the mongoose had won. He had encouraged it to live in the garden, to keep away the snakes, and fed it regularly with scraps from the kitchen. He had never tried taming it, because a wild mongoose was more useful than a domesticated one.

From the banyan tree I often saw the mongoose patrolling the four corners of the garden, and once I saw him with an egg in his mouth and knew he had been in the poultry house; but he hadn't harmed the birds, and I knew Grandmother would forgive him for stealing as long as he kept the snakes away.

The banyan tree was also the setting for what we were to call the Strange Case of the Grey Squirrel and the White Rat.

The white rat was Grandfather's—he had bought it from the

bazaar for four annas—but I would often take it with me into the banyan tree, where it soon struck up a friendship with one of the squirrels. They would go off together on little excursions among the roots and branches of the old tree.

Then the squirrel started building a nest. At first, she tried building it in my pockets, and when I went indoors and changed my clothes I would find straw and grass falling out. Then one day Grandmother's knitting was missing. We hunted for it everywhere but without success.

Next day I saw something glinting in the hole in the banyan tree and, going up to investigate, saw that it was the end of Grandmother's steel knitting needle. On looking further, I discovered that the hole was crammed with knitting. And amongst the wool were three baby squirrels—all of them white!

Grandfather had never seen white squirrels before, and we gazed at them in wonder. We were puzzled for some time, but when I mentioned the white rat's frequent visits to the tree, Grandfather told me that the rat must be the father. Rats and squirrels were related to each other, he said, and so it was quite possible for them to have offspring—in this case, white squirrels!

# Ghosts of the Savoy

The clock over the Savoy Bar is stationary at 8.20 and has been like that since the atomic bomb was dropped on Hiroshima fifty years ago. That's what Nandu tells me, and I have no reason to disbelieve him. Many of his more outlandish statements often turn out to be true.

Almost any story about this old hotel in Mussoorie has a touch of the improbable about it, even when supported by facts. A previous owner, Mr McClintock, had a false nose—according to Nandu, who never saw it. So I checked with old Negi, who first came to work in the hotel as a room boy back in 1932 (a couple of years before I was born) and who, sixty years and two wives later, looks after the front office. Negi tells me it's quite true.

'I used to take McClintock sahib his cup of cocoa last thing at night. After leaving his room I'd dash around to one of the windows and watch him until he went to bed. The last thing he did, before putting the light out, was to remove his false nose and place it on the bedside table. He never slept with it on. I suppose it bothered him whenever he turned over or slept on his face. First thing in the morning, before having his cup of tea, he'd put it on again. A great man, McClintock sahib.'

'But how did he lose his nose in the first place?' I asked.

'Wife bit it off,' said Nandu.

'No, sir,' said Negi, whose reputation for telling the truth is proverbial. 'It was shot away by a German bullet during World War I. He got the Victoria Cross as compensation.' 'And when he died, was he wearing his nose?' I asked.

'No, sir,' said old Negi, continuing his tale with some relish. 'One morning when I took the sahib his cup of tea, I found him stone dead, *without his nose*! It was lying on the bedside table. I suppose I should have left it there, but McClintock sahib was a good man, I could not bear to have the whole world knowing about his false nose. So I stuck it back on his face and then went and informed the manager. A natural death, just a sudden heart attack. But I made sure that he went into his coffin with his nose attached!'

We all agreed that Negi was a good man to have around, especially in a crisis.

Mr McClintock's ghost is supposed to haunt the corridors of the hotel, but I have yet to encounter it. Will the ghost be wearing its nose? Old Negi thinks not (the false nose being man-made), but then he hasn't seen the ghost at close quarters, only receding into the distance between the two giant deodars on the edge of the Beer Garden. Those deodars have been there a couple of hundred years, before the hotel was built, before the hill station came up.

A lot of people who enter the Bar look pretty far gone, and

sometimes I have difficulty distinguishing the living from the dead. But the real ghosts are those who manage to slip away without paying for their drinks.

I don't have to slip away. In the five or six years during which I have helped to prop up the Savoy Bar, I have seldom paid for a drink. That's the kind of friend I have in Nandu. You won't find a harsh word about him in these pages. I think he decided long ago that I was an adornment to the Bar, and that, draped over a bar stool, I looked like Ray Milland in *The Lost Weekend*. (He won an Oscar for that, remember?)

As for the Man-from-Sail, who is usually parked on the next bar stool, he's no adornment, in spite of the Jackie Shroff-moustache. But I have to admit that he's skilful at pouring drinks, mixing cocktails and showing tipsy ladies to the powder room. He doesn't pay for his drinks either.

How, then, does dear Nandu survive? Obviously there are some real customers in the wings, and we help them feel at home, chatting them up and encouraging them to try the Royal Salute or even a glass of Beaujolais. I can rattle off the history of the hotel for anyone who wants to hear it; and as for the Man-from-Sail, he provides a free ambulance service for those who can't handle the hotel's hospitality. The Man-from-Sail is the town's number one blood donor, so if you come away from your transfusion with a bad hangover, you'll know whose blood is coursing around in your veins. But it's real Scotch, not the stuff they make at the bottom of the Sail mountain.

Nandu tells me that Pearl Buck, the Nobel laureate, stayed here for a few days in the early fifties. I looked up the hotel register and found that he was right as usual. As far as I know,

Miss Buck did not record her impressions of the hotel or the town in any of her books. It's the sort of place people usually have something to say about. Like the correspondent of the *Melbourne Age* who complained because the roof had blown off his room during one of our equinoxal storms. A frivolous sort of complaint, to say the least. Nandu placated him by saying, 'Sir, in Delhi you can only get a five-star room. From your room here you can see all the stars!' And so he could, once the clouds had rolled away.

It's a windy sort of mountain, and in cyclonic storms our corrugated iron roofs are frequently blown away. Old Negi recalls that a portion of the Savoy roof once landed on the St George's School flat, five miles away, at the height of the midsummer storm. In its flight it decapitated an early-morning fitness freak. Had anyone else told me the story, I wouldn't have believed it. But Negi's word is the real thing—as good as a sip of Johnnie Walker Blue Label.

And here's a limerick I wrote for Nandu and the Man-from-Sail:

*There was a young man who could fix*
*Anything in five minutes or six;*
*His statue is found*
*On Savoy's hallowed ground,*
*With Nandu beside him, transfix'd!*

# In a Crystal Ball: A Mussoorie Mystery

Conan Doyle, the creator of Sherlock Holmes, had a lifelong interest in unusual criminal cases, and his friends often passed on to him interesting accounts of crime and detection from around the world. It was in this way that he learnt of the strange death of Miss Frances Garnett-Orme in the Indian hill station of Mussoorie. Here was a murder combining the weird borders of the occult with a crime mystery as inexplicable as any devised by Doyle himself.

In April 1912 (shortly before the *Titanic* went down), Conan Doyle received a letter from his Sussex neighbour Rudyard Kipling:

*Dear Doyle,*

*There has been a murder in India. A murder by suggestion at Mussoorie, which is one of the most curious things in its line on record.*

*Everything that is improbable and on the face of it impossible is in this case.*

Kipling had received details of the case from a friend working in the Allahabad *Pioneer*, a paper for which, as a young man, he had worked in the 1880s. Urging Doyle to pursue the story, Kipling concluded: 'The psychology alone is beyond description.'

Doyle was indeed interested to hear more, for India had furnished him with material in the past, as in *The Sign of Four* and several short stories. Kipling, too, had turned to crime and detection in his early stories of Strickland of the Indian Police. The two writers got together and discussed the case, which was indeed a fascinating affair.

The scene was set in Mussoorie, a popular hill station in the foothills of the Himalayas. It wasn't as grand as Simla (where the Viceroy and his entourage went) but it was a charming and convivial place, with a number of hotels and boarding houses, a small military cantonment, and several private schools for European children.

It was during the summer 'season' of 1911 that Miss Frances Garnett-Orme came to stay in Mussoorie, taking a suite at the Savoy, a popular resort hotel. On 28 July she celebrated her 49th birthday. She was the daughter of George Garnett-Orme, of Skipton-in-Craven in Yorkshire, a district registrar of the Country Court. It was a family important enough to be counted among the landed gentry. Her father had died in 1892.

She came out to India in 1893 with the intention of marrying Jack Grant of the United Provinces Police. But he died in 1894 and she went back to England. Upset by his death following so soon after her father's, she turned to spiritualism in the hope of communicating with him. We must remember that spiritualism was all the rage in the early years of the century, seances and table-rappings being part of the social scene both in England and India. Madam Blavatsky, the chief exponent of spiritualism, was probably at the height of her popularity around this time; she spent her 'seasons' in neighbouring Simla, where she had many followers.

Miss Garnett-Orme's life was unsettled. She was drawn back to India, returning in 1901 to live in Lucknow, the regional capital of the United Provinces. She was still in contact with Jack Grant's family and saw his brother occasionally. The summer of 1907 was spent at Nainital, a hill station popular with Lucknow residents. It was here that she met Miss Eva Mountstephen, who was working as a governess.

Eva Mountstephen, too, had an interest in spiritualism. It appears that she had actually told several of her friends about this time that she had learnt (in the course of a seance) that in 1911 she would come into a great deal of money.

We are told that there was something sinister about Miss Mountstephen. She specialized in crystal-gazing, and what she saw in the glass often took a violent form. Her 'control', that is her connection in the spirit world, was a dead friend named Mrs Winter.

As a result of their common interest in the occult, Miss Garnett-Orme took on the younger woman as a companion when she returned to Lucknow in the winter. There they settled down together. But the summers were spent at one of the various hill stations. Was there a latent lesbianism in their relationship? It was a restless, rootless life, but they were held together by the strong and heady influence of the seance table and the crystal ball. Miss Garnett-Orme's indifferent health also made her dependent on the younger woman.

In the summer of 1911, the couple went up to Mussoorie, probably the most frivolous of hill stations, where 'seasonal' love affairs were almost the order of the day. They took rooms in the Savoy. Electricity had yet to reach Mussoorie, and it was still the age of candelabras and gas-lit streets. Every house had a grand piano. If you didn't go out to a ball, you sang or danced at home. But Miss Garnett-Orme's spiritual pursuits took precedence over these more mundane entertainments. Towards the end of the 'season', on 12 September, Miss Mountstephen returned to Lucknow to pack up their household for a move to Jhansi, where they planned to spend the winter.

On the morning of 19 September, while Miss Mountstephen was still away, Miss Garnett-Orme was found dead in her bed. The door was locked from the inside. On her bedside table was a glass. She was positioned on the bed as though laid out by a nurse or undertaker.

Because of these puzzling circumstances, Major Birdwood of the Indian Medical Service (who was the Civil Surgeon in Mussoorie) was called in. He decided to hold an autopsy. It was discovered that Miss Garnett-Orme had been poisoned with prussic acid.

Prussic acid is a quick-acting poison, and would have killed too quickly for the victim to have composed herself in the way she was found. An ayah told the police that she had seen someone (she could not tell whether it was a man or a woman) slipping away through a large skylight and escaping over the roof.

Hill stations are hotbeds of rumour and intrigue, and of

course the gossips had a field day. Miss Garnett-Orme suffered from dyspepsia and was always dosing herself from a large bottle of Sodium Bicarbonate, which was regularly refilled. It was alleged that the bottle had been tampered with, that an unknown white powder had been added. Her doctor was questioned thoroughly. They even questioned a touring mind-reader, Mr Alfred Capper, who claimed that Miss Mountstephen had hurried from a room rather than have her mind read!

After several weeks the police arrested Miss Mountstephen. Although she had a convincing alibi (due to her absence in Jhansi) the police sought to prove that some kind of sinister influence had been exerted on Miss Garnett-Orme to take her medicine at a particular time. Thus, through suggestion, the murderer could kill and yet be away at the time of death. In her first novel, *The Mysterious Affair at Styles* (1920), the poisoner was in a distant place by the time her victim reached the fatal dose, the poison having precipitated to the bottom of the mixture. Perhaps Miss Christie read accounts of the Garnett-Orme case in the British press. Even the motive was similar.

But there was no Hercule Poirot in Mussoorie, and in court this theory could never be made convincing. The police case was never strong (they would have done better to have followed the ayah's lead), and it appears that they only acted because there was considerable ill-feeling in Mussoorie against Miss Mountstephen.

When the trial came up at Allahabad in March 1912, it caused a sensation. Murder by remote control was something new in the annals of crime. But after hearing many days of evidence about the ladies' way of life, about crystal-gazing and premonitions of death, the court found Miss Mountstephen innocent. The Chief Justice, in delivering his verdict, remarked that the true circumstances of Miss Garnett-Orme's death would probably never be known. And he was right.

Miss Mountstephen applied for probate of her friend's will. But the Garnett-Orme family in England sent out her brother, Mr Hunter Garnett-Orme, to contest it. The case went in favour of Mr Garnett-Orme. The District Judge (W.D. Burkitt) turned down Miss Mountstephen's application on grounds of 'fraud and undue influence in connection with spiritualism and crystal-gazing'. She went in appeal to the Allahabad High Court, but the Lower Court's decision was upheld.

Miss Mountstephen returned to England. We do not know her state of mind, but if she was innocent, she must have been a deeply embittered woman. Miss Garnett-Orme's doctor lost his flourishing practice in Mussoorie and left the country too. There were rumours that he and Miss Mountstephen had conspired to get hold of Miss Garnett-Orme's considerable fortune.

There was one more puzzling feature of the case. Mr Charles Jackson, a painter friend of many of those involved, had died suddenly, apparently of cholera, two months after Miss Garnett-Orme's mysterious death. The police took an interest in his sudden demise. When he was exhumed on 23 December, the body was found to be in a perfect state of preservation. He had died of arsenic poisoning.

Murder or suicide? This puzzle, too, was never resolved. Was there a connection with Miss Garnett-Orme's death? That too we shall never know. Had Conan Doyle taken up Kipling's suggestion and involved himself in the case (as he had done in so many others in England), perhaps the outcome would have been different.

As it is, we can only make our own conjectures.

# Up at Sisters Bazaar

A few years ago I spent a couple of summers up at Sisters Bazaar, at the farthest extremity of Mussoorie's Landour cantonment—an area as yet untouched by the tentacles of a bulging, disoriented octopus of a hill station.

There were a number of residences up at Sisters, most of them old houses, but they were at some distance from each other, separated by clumps of oak or stands of deodar. After sundown, flying foxes swooped across the roads, and the nightjar set up its nocturnal chant. Here, I thought, I would live like Thoreau at Walden Pond—alone, aloof, far from the strife and cacophony of the vast amusement park that was now Mussoorie. How wrong I was proved to be!

To begin with, I found that almost everyone on the hillside was busily engaged in writing a book. Was the atmosphere really so conducive to creative activity, or was it just a conspiracy to put me out of business? The discovery certainly put me out of my stride completely, and it was several weeks before I could write a word.

There was a retired Brigadier who was writing a novel about World War II, and a retired Vice Admiral who was writing a book about a Rear Admiral. Mrs S, who had been an actress in the early days of the talkies, was writing poems in the manner of Wordsworth; and an ageing (or rather, resurrected) ex-Maharani was penning her memoirs. There was also an elderly American who wrote salacious bestselling novels about India. It was said of him that he looked like Hemingway and wrote like Charles Bronson.

With all this frenzied literary activity going on around me, it wasn't surprising that I went into shock for some time.

I was saved (or so I thought) by a 'far-out' ex-hippie and ex-Hollywood scriptwriter who decided he would produce a children's film based on one of my stories. It was a pleasant little story, and all would have gone well if our producer friend hadn't returned from some high-altitude poppy fields in a bit of a trance and failed to notice that his leading lady was in the family way. Although the events of the story all took place in a single day, the film itself took about four months to complete, with the result that her figure altered considerably from scene to scene until, by late evening of the same day, she was displaying all the glories of imminent motherhood.

Naturally, the film was never released. I believe our producer friend now runs a health-food restaurant in Sydney. I shared a large building (it had paper-thin walls) with several other tenants, one of whom, a French girl in her thirties, was learning to play the sitar. She and her tabla-playing companion would sleep by day, but practise all through the night, making sleep impossible for me or anyone else in my household. I would try singing operatic arias to drown her out, but you can't sing all night and she always outlasted me. Even a raging forest fire, which forced everyone else to evacuate the building for a night, did not keep her from her sitar any more than Rome burning kept Nero from his fiddle. Finally I got one of the chowkidar's children to pour sand into her instrument, and that silenced her for some time.

Another tenant who was there for a short while was a Dutchman, (yes, we were a cosmopolitan lot in the 1980s, before visa regulations were tightened) who claimed to be an acupuncturist. He showed me his box of needles and promised to cure me of the headaches that bothered me from time to time. But before he could start the treatment, he took a tumble while coming home from a late night party and fell down the khud into a clump of cacti, the sharp pointed kind, which punctured the more tender parts of his anatomy. He had to spend a couple of weeks in the local mission hospital, receiving more conventional treatment, and he never did return to cure my headaches.

How did Sisters Bazaar come by its name?

Well, in the bad old, good old days, when Landour was a convalescent station for sick and weary British soldiers, the nursing sisters had their barracks in the long, low building that lines the road opposite Prakash's Store. On the old maps this building is called The Sisters. For a time it belonged to Dev Anand's family, but I believe it has since changed hands.

Of a 'bazaar' there is little evidence, although Prakash's Store must be at least a hundred years old. It is famous for its home-made cheese, and tradition has it that several generations of the Nehru family have patronized the store, from Motilal

Nehru in the 1920s, to Rahul and his mother in more recent times.

I am more of a jam-fancier myself, and although I no longer live in the area, I do sometimes drop into the store for a can of raspberry or apricot or plum jam, made from the fruit brought here from the surrounding villages.

Further down the road is Dahlia Bank, where dahlias once covered the precipitous slope (known as the 'Eyebrow'), behind the house. The old military hospital (which was opened in 1827), has been altered and expanded to house the present Defence Institute of Work Study. Beyond it lies Mount Hermon, with the lonely grave of a lady who perished here one wild and windy winter, 150 years ago. And close by lies the lovely Oakville Estate, where at least three generations of the multi-talented Alter fancily have lived. They do everything from acting in Hindi films to climbing greasy poles, Malkhumb-style. From wise old Bob to Steve and Andy, those Alter boys are mighty handy.

It is cold up there in winter, and I now live about 500 feet lower down, where it is only slightly warmer. But my walks take me up the hill from time to time. Most of the unusual eccentric people I have written about have gone away, but others, equally interesting, have taken their place. But for news of them you'll have to wait for my autobiography. The Mussoorie gossips will then get a dose of their own medicine. Let them start having sleepless nights.

# Miss Bun and Others

*1 March 1975*

Beer in the sun. High in the spruce tree the barbet calls, heralding summer. A few puffy clouds drift lazily over the mountains. Is this the great escape?

I could sit here all day soaking up beer and sunshine, but at some time during the day I must wipe the dust from my typewriter and produce something readable. There's only eight hundred rupees in the bank, book sales are falling off, and magazines are turning away from fiction.

Prem spoils me, giving me rice and kofta curry for lunch, which means that I sleep till four when Miss Bun arrives with patties and samosas.

Miss Bun is the baker's daughter.

Of course that's not her real name. Her real name is very long and beautiful, but I won't give it here for obvious reasons and also because her brother is big and ugly.

I am seeing Miss Bun after two months. She's been with relatives in Bareilly.

She sits at the foot of my bed, absolutely radiant. Her raven-black hair lies loose on her shoulders, her eyelashes have been trimmed and blackened and so have her eyes, with kajal. Her eyes, so large and innocent—and calculating!

There are pretty glass bangles on her wrists and she wears a pair of new slippers. Her kameez is new too—green silk, with gold embroidered sleeves.

'You must have a rich lover,' I remark, taking her hand and gently pulling her towards me. 'Who gave you all this finery?'

'You did. Don't you remember? Before I went away, you gave me a hundred rupees.'

'That was for the train and bus fares, I thought.'

'Oh, my uncle paid the fares. So I bought myself these things. Are they nice?'

'Very pretty. And so are you. If you were ten years older and I ten years younger, we'd make a good pair. But I'd have been broke long before this!'

She giggles and drops a paper bag full of samosas on the bedside table. I hate samosas and patties, but I keep ordering them because it gives Miss Bun a pretext for visiting me. It's all in the way of helping the bakery get by. When she goes, I give the lot to Bijju and Binya or whoever might be passing.

'You've been away a long time,' I complain. 'What if I'd got married while you were away?'

'Then you'd stop ordering samosas.'

'Or get them from that old man Bashir, who makes much better ones, and cheaper!'

She drops her head on my shoulder. Her hair is heavily scented with jasmine hair oil, and I nearly pass out. They should use it instead of anaesthesia.

'You smell very nice,' I lie. 'Do I get a kiss?'

She gives me a long kiss, as though to make up for her long absence. Her kisses always have a nice wholesome flavour, as you would expect from someone who lives in a bakery.

'That was an expensive kiss.'

'I want to buy some face cream.'

'You don't need face cream. Your complexion is perfect. It must be the good quality flour you use in the bakery.'

'I don't put flour on my face. Anyway, I want the cream for my elder sister. She has pockmarks.'

I surrender and give her two fives, quickly putting away my wallet.

'And when will you pay for the samosas?'

'Next week.'

'I'll bring you something nice next week,' she says, pausing in the doorway.

'Well, thanks, I was getting tired of samosas.'

She was gone in a twinkling.

I'll say this for Miss Bun—she doesn't trouble to hide her intentions.

*March 4*

My policeman calls on me this morning. Ghanshyam, the constable attached to the Barlowganj outpost.

He is not very tall for a policeman, and he has a round, cheerful countenance, which is unusual in his profession. He looks smart in his uniform. Most constables prefer to hang around in their pyjamas most of the time.

Nothing alarming about Ghanshyam's visit. He comes to see me about once a week, and has been doing so ever since I spent a night in the police station last year.

It happened when I punched a Muzzaffarnagar businessman in the eye for bullying a rickshaw coolie. The fat slob very naturally lodged a complaint against me, and that same evening a sub-inspector called and asked me to accompany him to the thana. It was too late to arrange anything and in any case I had only been taken in for questioning, so I had to spend the night at the police post. The sub-inspector went home and left me in the charge of a constable. A wooden bench and a charpoy were the only items of furniture in my cell, if you could call it that. The charpoy was meant for the night-duty constable, but he very generously offered it to me.

'But where will you sleep?' I asked.

'Oh, I don't feel like sleeping. Usually I go to the night show at the Picture Palace, but I suppose I'll have to stay here because of you.'

He looked rather sulky. Obviously I'd ruined his plans for the night.

'You don't have to stay because of me,' I said. 'I won't tell the SHO. You go to the Picture Palace, I'll look after the thana.'

He brightened up considerably, but still looked a bit doubtful.

'You can trust me,' I said encouragingly. 'My grandfather was a private soldier who became a Buddhist.'

'Then I can trust you as far as your grandfather.' He was

quite cheerful now, and sent for two cups of tea from the shop across the road. It came gratis, of course. A little later he left me, and I settled down on the cot and slept fitfully. The constable came back during the early hours and went to sleep on the bench. Next morning I was allowed to go home. The Muzzaffarnagar businessman had got into another fight and was lodged in the main thana. I did not hear about the matter again.

Ghanshyam, the constable, having struck up a friendship with me, was to visit me from time to time.

And here he is today, boots shining, teeth gleaming, cheeks almost glowing, far too charming a person to be a policeman.

'Hello, Ghanshyam bhai,' I welcome him. 'Sit down and have some tea.'

'No, I can't stop for long,' he says, but sits down beside me on the verandah steps. 'Can you do me a favour?'

'Sure. What is it?'

'I'm fed up with Barlowganj. I want to get a transfer.'

'And how can I help you? I don't know any netas or bigwigs.'

'No, but our SP will be here next week and he can have me transferred. Will you speak to him?'

'But why should he listen to me?'

'Well, you see, he has a weakness...'

'We all have our weaknesses. Does your SP have a weakness similar to mine? Do we proceed to blackmail him?'

'Yes. You see, he writes poetry. And you are a kavi, a poet, aren't you?'

'At times,' I concede. 'And I have to admit it's a weakness, especially as no one cares to read my poetry.'

'No one reads the SP's poetry, either. Although we have to

listen to it sometimes. When he has finished reading out one of his poems, we salute and say "Shabash!"'

'A captive audience. I wish I had one.'

Ignoring my sarcasm, Ghanshyam continues: 'The trouble is, he can't get anyone to publish his poems. This makes him bad tempered and unsympathetic to applications for transfer. Can you help?'

'I am not a publisher. I can only salute like the rest of you.'

'But you know publishers, don't you? If you can get some of his poems published, he'd be very grateful. To you. To me. To both of us!'

'You really are an optimist.'

'Just one or two poems. You see, I've already told him about you. How you spent all night in the lock-up writing verses. He thinks you are a famous writer. He's depending on me now. If his poems get published he will give me a transfer. I'm sick of Barlowganj!' He gives me a hug and pinches me on the cheek.

Before he can go any further, I say: 'Well, I'll do my best'—I am thinking of a little magazine published in Bhopal where most of my rejects find a home. 'For your sake, I'll try. But first I must see the poems.'

'You shall even see the SP,' he promises. 'I'll bring him here next week. You can give him a cup of tea.'

He gets up, gives me a smart salute and goes up the path with a spring in his step. The sort of man who knows how to get his transfers and promotions in a perfectly honest manner.

*March 7*

It gets warmer day by day.

This morning I decided to sunbathe—quite modestly, of course. Retaining my old khaki shorts but removing all other clothing, I stretched out on a mattress in the garden. Almost immediately I was disturbed by the baker (Miss Bun's father for a change), who presented me with two loaves of bread and half a dozen chocolate pastries, ordered the previous day. Then Prem's small son, Raki, turned up, demanding a pastry, and I gave him two. He insisted on joining me on the mattress, where he proceeded to drop crumbs in my hair and on my chest. 'Good morning, Mr Bond!' came the dulcet tones of Mrs Biggs, leaning over the gate. Forgetting that she was short-sighted, I jumped to my feet, and at the same time my shorts slipped down over my knees. As I grabbed for them, Mrs Biggs's effusiveness reached greater heights. 'Why, what a lovely *agapanthus* you've got!' she exclaimed, referring no doubt to the solitary lily in the garden. I must confess I blushed. Then, recovering myself, I returned her greeting, remarking on the freshness of the morning.

Mrs Biggs, at eighty, was a little deaf as well, and replied, 'I'm very well, thank you, Mr Bond. Is that a child you're carrying?'

'Yes, Prem's small son.'

'Prem is your son? I didn't know you had a family.' At this point Raki decided to pluck the spectacles off Mrs Biggs's nose, and after I had recovered them for her, she beat a hasty retreat. Later, the Rev. Mr Biggs came over to borrow a book.

'Just light reading,' he said. 'I can't concentrate for long periods.'

He has become extremely absent-minded and forgetful; one of the drawbacks of living to an advanced age. During a funeral last year at which he took the funeral service, he read out the service for Burial at Sea. It was raining heavily at the time, and no one seemed to notice.

Now he has borrowed two of my Ross Macdonalds—the same two he read last month. I refrained from pointing this out. If he has forgotten the books already, it won't matter if he reads them again.

Having spent the better part of his seventy-odd years in India, the Rev. Biggs has a lot of stories to tell, his favourite being the one about the crocodile he shot in Orissa when he was a young man. He'd pitched his tent on the banks of a river and gone to sleep on a camp cot. During the night he felt his cot moving, and before he could gather his wits, the cot had moved swiftly through the opening of the tent and was rapidly making its way down to the river. Mr Biggs leapt for dry land while the cot, firmly wedged on the back of the crocodile, disappeared into the darkness.

Crocodiles, it seems, often bury themselves in the mud when they go to sleep, and Mr Biggs had pitched his tent and made his bed on top of a sleeping crocodile. Waking in the night, it had made for the nearest water.

Mr Biggs shot it the following morning—or so he would have us believe—the crocodile having reappeared on the river bank with the cot still attached to its back.

Now having told me this story for the umpteenth time, Biggs said he really must be going, and returning to the bookshelf, extracted Gibbons' *Decline and Fall of the Roman Empire,* having forgotten the Ross Macdonalds on a side table.

'I must do some serious reading,' he said. 'These modern novels are so violent.'

'Lots of violence in *Decline and Fall*,' I remarked.

'Ah, but it's history, isn't it? Well, I must go now, Mr Macdonald. Mustn't waste your time.'

As he stepped outside, he collided with Miss Bun, who dropped samosas all over the verandah steps.

'Oh, dear, I'm so sorry,' he apologized, and started picking up the samosas despite my attempts to prevent him from doing so. He then took the paper bag from Miss Bun and replaced the samosas.

'And who is this little girl?' he said benignly, patting Miss Bun on the head. 'One of your nieces?'

'That's right, sir. My favourite niece.'

'Well, I must not keep you. Service as usual, on Sunday.'

'Right, Mr Biggs.'

I have never been to a local church service, but why disillusion Rev. Biggs? I shall defend everyone's right to go to a place of worship provided they allow me the freedom to stay away.

Miss Bun was staring after Rev. Biggs as he crossed the road. Her mouth was slightly agape. 'What's the matter?' I asked.

'He's taken all the samosas!'

When I kiss Miss Bun, she bites my lip and draws blood.

'What was that for?' I complain.

'Just to make you angry.'

'But I don't like getting angry.'

'That's why.'

I get angry just to please her, and we take a tumble on the carpet.

*March 11*

Does anyone here make money? Apart from the traders, of course, who tuck it all away ...

A young man turned up yesterday, selling geraniums. He had a bag full of geraniums—cuttings and whole plants.

'All colours,' he told me confidently. 'Only one rupee a cutting.'

'I can buy them much cheaper at the government nursery.'

'But you would have to walk there, sir—six miles! I have brought these to your very doorstep. I will plant them for you in your empty ghee tins at no extra cost!'

'That's all right, you can give me a few. But what makes you sell geraniums?'

'I have nothing to eat, sir. I haven't eaten for two days.'

He must have sold all his plants that day, because in the evening I saw him at the country liquor shop, tippling away—and all on an empty stomach, I presume!

*March 12*

Mrs Biggs tells me that someone slipped into her garden yesterday morning while she was out, and removed all her geraniums!

'The most honest of people won't hesitate to steal flowers—or books,' I remark carelessly. 'Never mind, Mrs Biggs, you can have some of my geraniums. I bought them yesterday.'

'That's extremely kind of you, Mr Bond. And you've only just put them down, I can tell,' she says, spotting the cuttings in the Dalda tins. 'No, I couldn't deprive you—'

'I'll get you some,' I offer, and generously surrender half the geraniums, vowing that if ever I come across that young man again, I'll get him to recover all the plants he sold elsewhere.

*March 19*

Vinod, now selling newspapers, arrives as I am pouring myself a beer under the cherry tree. It's a warm day and I can see he is thirsty.

'Can I have a drink of water?' he asks.

'Would you like some beer?'

'Yes, *sir!*'

As I have an extra bottle, I pour him a glass and he squats on the grass near the old wall and brings me up to date on the local gossip. There are about fifty papers in his shoulder hag, yet to be delivered.

'You may feel drowsy after some time,' I warn. 'Don't leave your papers in the wrong houses.'

'Nothing to worry about,' he says, emptying the glass and gazing fondly at the bottle sparkling in the spring sunshine.

'Have some more,' I tell him, and go indoors to see what Prem is making for lunch. (Stuffed gourds, fried brinjal slices and pilaf. Prem is in a good mood, preparing my favourite dishes. When I upset him, he gives me string beans.) Returning to the garden, I find Vinod well into his second glass of beer. Half of Barlowganj and all of jharipani (the next village) are snarling and cursing, waiting for their newspapers.

'Your customers must be getting impatient,' I remark. 'Surely they want to know the result of the cricket test.' 'Oh, they heard it on the radio. This is the morning edition. I can deliver it in the evening.'

I go indoors and have my lunch with little Raki, and ask Prem to give Vinod something to eat. When I come outside again, he is stretched out under the cherry tree, burping contentedly.

'Thank you for the lunch,' be says, and closes his eyes and goes to sleep.

He's gone by evening but his bag of papers rests against my front door.

'He's left his papers behind,' I remark to Prem.

'Oh, he'll deliver them tomorrow, along with tomorrow's paper. He'll say the mail bus was late due to a landslide.'

In the evening I walk through the old bazaar and linger in front of a Tibetan shop, gazing at the brassware, coloured stones, amulets, masks. I am about to pass on, when I catch a glimpse of the girl who looks after the shop. Two soft brown eyes in a round jade-smooth face. A hesitant smile.

I step inside. I have never cared much for Tibetan handicrafts, but beautiful brown eyes are different.

'Can I look around? I want to buy a present for a friend.'

I look around. She helps me by displaying bangles, necklaces, rings—all on the assumption that my friend is a young lady.

I choose the more frightening of two devil masks, and promise to come again for the pair to it.

On the way home I meet Miss Bun.

'When shall I come?' she asks, pirouetting on the road.

'Next year.'

'Next year!' Her pretty mouth falls open.

'That's right,' I say. 'You've just lost the election.'

*March 31*

Miss Bun hasn't been for several days. This morning I find her washing clothes at the public tap. She gives me a quick smile as I pass.

'It's nice to see you hard at work,' I remark.

She looks quickly to left and right, then says, 'It's punishment, because I bought new bangles with the money you gave me.'

I hurry on down the road.

During the afternoon siesta I am roused by someone knocking on the door. A slim boy with thick hair and bushy eyebrows is standing there. I don't know him, but his eyes remind me of someone.

He tells me he is Miss Bun's older brother. At a guess, he would be only a year or two older than her.

'Come in,' I say. It's best to be friendly! What could he possibly want?

He produces a bag of samosas and puts them down on my bedside table.

'My sister cannot come this week. I will bring you samosas instead. Is that all right?'

'Oh, sure. Sit down, sit down. So you're Master Bun. It's nice to know you.'

He sits down on the edge of the bed and studies the picture on the wall—a print of Kurosawa's *Wave.*

'Shall I pay you now for the samosas?' I ask.

'No, no, whenever you like.'

'And do you go to school or college?'

'No, I help my father in the bakery. Are you ill, sir?'

'No. What makes you think so?'

'Because you were lying down.'

'Well, I like lying down. It's. better than standing up. And I do get a headache if I read or write for too long.'

He offers to give me a head massage, and I submit to his ministrations for about five minutes. The headache is now much worse, but I pay for both massage and samosas and tell him he can come again—preferably next year.

My next visitor is Constable Ghanshyam Singh, who tells me that the SP has extracted confessions from a couple of thieves simply by making them stand for hours and listen to him reciting his poetry. I know our police have a reputation for torturing suspects, but I think this is carrying things a bit too far.

'And what about your transfer?' I ask.

'As soon as those poems are published in the *Weekly*.'

'I'll do my best,' I promise.

(They appeared in the Bhopal *Weekly*. And a year later, when I was editing *Imprint*, I was able to publish one of the SP's poems. He has always maintained that if I'd published more of them, the magazine would never have folded.)

*A note on Miss Bun*
*Little Miss Bun is fond of bed,*
*But she keeps a cash box in her head.*

*April 8*

Rev. Biggs at the door, book in hand.

'I won't take up your time, Mr Bond. But I thought it was time I returned your butterfly book.'

'My butterfly book?'

'Yes, thank you very much. I enjoyed it a great deal.'

Mr Biggs hands me the book on butterflies, a handsomely illustrated volume. It isn't my book, but if Mr Biggs insists on giving me someone else's book, who am I to quibble? He'd never find the right owner, anyway.

'By the way, have you seen Mrs Biggs?' he asks.

'No, not this morning, sir.'

'She went off without telling me. She's always doing things like that. Very irritating.'

After he has gone, I glance at the fly leaf of the book. It says W. Biggs. So it's one of his own...

A little later Mrs Biggs comes by.

'Have you seen Will?' she asks.

'He was here about fifteen minutes ago. He was looking for you.'

'Oh, he knew I'd gone to the garden shed. How tiresome! I suppose he's wandered off somewhere.'

'Never mind, Mrs Biggs, he'll make his way home when he gets hungry. A good lunch will always bring a wanderer home. By the way, I've got his book on butterflies. Perhaps you'd return it to him for me? And he shouldn't lend it to just anyone, you know. It's a valuable book, you don't want to lose it.'

'I'm sure it was quite safe with you, Mr Bond.'

Books always are, of course. On principle, I never steal another man's books. I might take his geraniums or his old school tie, but I wouldn't deprive him of his books. Or the song or melody or dream be lives by. And here's a little lullaby for Raki:

*Little one, don't be afraid of this big river.*
*Be safe in these warm arms for ever.*
*Grow tall, my child, be wise and strong.*
*But do not take from any man his song.*
*Little one, don't be afraid of this dark night.*
*Walk boldly as you see the truth and light.*
*Love well, my child, laugh all day long,*
*But do not take from any man his song.*

*April 16*

Is there something about the air at this height that makes people light-headed, absent-minded? Ten years from now I will probably be as forgetful as Mr Biggs. I must climb the next mountain before I forget where it is.

Outline for a story.

Someone lives in a small hut near a spring, within sound of running water. He never leaves the place, except to walk into the town for books, post, and supplies. 'Don't you ever get bored here?' I ask. 'Do you never wish to leave?' 'No,' he replies, and tells me of his experience in the desert, when for two days and two nights (the limit of human endurance in regard to thirst), he went without water. On the second night, half dead, lying in the open beneath the stars, he dreamt of just such a spring in the mountains, and it was as though it gave him spiritual sustenance. So later, when he was fully recovered, he went in search of the spring (which he was sure existed), and found it while hiking in the Himalayas. He knew that as long as he remained by the spring he would never feel unsafe; it was where his guardian spirit lived...

And so I feel safe near my own spring, my own mountain, for this is where my guardian spirit lives too.

*April 16*

Visited the Tibetan shop and bought a small brass vase encrusted with pretty stones.

I'd no intention of buying anything, but the girl smiled at me as I passed, and then I just had to go in; and once in, I couldn't just stand there, a fatuous grin on my face.

I had to buy something. And a vase is always a good thing to buy. If you don't like it, you can give it away.

If she smiles at me every time I pass, I shall probably build up a collection of vases.

She isn't a girl, really; she's probably about thirty. I suppose she has a husband who smuggles Chinese goods in from Nepal, while her children—'charity cases'—go to one of the posh public schools. But she's fresh and pretty, and then, of course, I don't have many young women smiling at me these days. I shall be forty-three next month.

*April 17*

Miss Bun still smiles at me, even though I frown at her when we pass.

This afternoon she brought me samosas and a rose.

'Where's your brother?' I asked gruffly. 'He has more to talk about.'

'He's busy in the bakery. See, I've brought you a rose.'

'How much did it cost?'

'Don't be silly. It's a present.'

'Thanks. I didn't know you grew roses.'

'I don't. It's from the school garden.'

'Well, thank you anyway. You actually stole something on my behalf!'

'Where shall I put it?'

I found my new vase, filled it with fresh water, placed the rose in it and set it down on my dressing table.

'It leaks,' remarked Miss Bun.

'My vase?' I was incredulous.

'See, the water's spreading all over your nice table.'

She was right, of course. Water from the bottom of the vase was running across the varnished wood of great-grandmother's old rosewood dressing table. The stain, I felt sure, would be permanent.

'But it's a new vase!' I protested.

'Someone must have cheated you. Why did you buy it without looking properly?'

'Well, you see, I didn't buy it actually. Someone gave it to me as a present.'

I fumed inwardly, vowing never again to visit the brassware shop. Never trust a smiling woman! I prefer Miss Bun's scowl.

'Do you want the vase?' she asks.

'No. Take it away.'

She places the rose on my pillow, throws the water out of the window and drops the vase into her cloth shopping bag.

'What will you do with it?' I ask.

'I'll seal the leak with flour,' she says.

*April 21*

A clear fresh morning after a week of intermittent rain. And what a morning for birds! Three doves courting, a cuckoo calling, a bunch of minas squabbling, and a pair of king crows doing Swedish exercises.

I find myself doing exercises of an original nature, devised by Master Bun. These consist of various contortions of the limbs which, he says, are good for my sex drive.

'But I don't want a sex drive,' I tell him. 'I want something that will take my mind *off* sex.'

So he gives me another set of exercises which consist mostly of deep breathing.

'Try holding your breath for five minutes,' he suggests.

'I know of someone who committed suicide by doing just that.'

'Then hold it for two minutes.'

I take a deep breath and last only a minute.

'No good,' he says. 'You have to relax more.'

'Well, I am tired of trying to relax. It doesn't work this way. What I need is a good meal.'

And Prem obliges by serving up my favourite kofta curry and rice. Satiated, I have no problem in relaxing for the rest of the afternoon.

*April 28*

Master Bun wears a troubled expression.

'It's about my sister,' he says.

'What about her?' I ask, fearing the worst.

'She has run away.'

'That's bad. On her own?'

'No... With a professor.'

'That should be all right. Professors are usually respectable people. Maths or English?'

'I don't know. He has a wife and children.'

'Then obviously he hasn't taken them along.'

'He has taken her to Roorkee. My sister is an innocent girl.'

'Well, there is a certain innocence about her,' I say, recalling Nobokov's *Lolita*. 'Maybe the professor wants to adopt her.'

'But she's a virgin.'

'Then she must be rescued! Why are you here, talking to me about it, when you should be rushing down to Roorkee?'

'That's why I've come. Can you lend me the bus fare?'

'Better still, I'll come with you. We must rescue the professor—sorry, I mean your sister!'

*May 1*

> —*Roorkee, to Roorkee, to find a sweet girl,*
> *Home again, home again, oh, what a whirl!*

We did everything except find Miss Bun. Our first evening in Roorkee we roamed the bazaar and the canal banks; the second day we did the rounds of the university, the regimental barracks and the headquarters of the Boys' Brigade. We made inquiries from all the bakers in Roorkee (many of them known to Master Bun), but none of them had seen his sister. On the college campus we asked for the professor, but no one had heard of him either.

Finally, we bought platform tickets and sat down on a bench at the end of the railway platform and watched the arrival and departure of trains, and the people who got on and off; we saw no one who looked in the least like Miss Bun. Master Bun bought an astrological guide from the station bookstall and studied his sister's horoscope to see if that might help, but it didn't. At the same bookstall, hidden under a pile of pirated Harold Robbins novels, I found a book of mine that had been published ten years earlier. No one had bought it in all that time. I replaced it at the top of the pile. Never lose hope!

On the third day we returned to Barlowganj and found Miss Bun at home.

She had gone no further than Debra's Paltan Bazaar, it seemed, and had ditched the professor there, having first made him buy her three dress pieces, two pairs of sandals, a sandalwood hair brush, a bottle of scent, and a satchel for her school books.

*May 5*

And now it's Mr Biggs's turn to disappear.

'Have you seen our Will?' asks Mrs Biggs at my gate.

'Not this morning, Mrs Biggs.'

'I can't find him anywhere. At breakfast he said he was going out for a walk, but nobody knows where he went, and he isn't in the school compound, I've just inquired. He's been gone over three hours!'

'Don't worry, Mrs Biggs. He'll turn up. Someone on the hillside must have asked him in for a cup of tea, and he's sitting there talking about the crocodile he shot in Orissa.'

But at lunchtime Mr Biggs hadn't returned; and that was alarming, because Mr Biggs had never been known to miss his favourite egg curry and pilaf.

We organized a search. Prem and I walked the length of the Barlowganj bazaar and even lodged an unofficial report with Constable Ghanshyam. No one had seen him in the bazaar. Several members of the school staff combed the hillside without picking up the scent.

Mid-afternoon, while giving my negative report to Mrs Biggs, I heard a loud thumping coming from the direction of her storeroom.

'What's all that noise downstairs?' I asked.

'Probably rats. I don't hear anything.'

I ran downstairs and opened the storeroom door, and there was Mr Biggs looking very dusty and very disgruntled. He wanted to know why the devil (the first time he'd taken the devil's name in vain) Mrs Biggs had shut him up for hours. He'd gone into the storeroom in search of an old walking stick, and Mrs Biggs, seeing the door open, had promptly bolted it, failing to hear her husband's cries for immediate release. But for Mr Bond's presence of mind, he averred, he might have been discovered years later, a mere skeleton!

The cook was still out hunting for him, so Mr Biggs had his egg curry cold. Still in a foul mood, he sat down and wrote a letter to his sister in Tunbridge Wells, asking her to send over a hearing aid for Mrs Biggs.

Constable Ghanshyam turned up in the evening to inform me that Mr Biggs had last been seen at Rajpur in the foothills, in the company of several gypsies!

'Never mind,' I said. 'These old men get that way. One last fling, one last romantic escapade, one last tilt at the windmill. If you have a dream, Ghanshyam, don't let them take it away from you.'

He looked puzzled, but went on to tell me that he was being transferred to Bareilly jail, where they keep those who have been found guilty but of unsound mind. It's a reward, no doubt, for his services in getting the SP's poems published. These journal entries date back some twenty years. What happened to Miss Bun? Well, she finally opened a beauty parlour in New Delhi, but I still can't tell you where it is, or give you her name.

Two or three years later, Mrs Biggs was laid to rest near her old friends in the Mussoorie cemetery. Rev. Biggs was flown home to Tunbridge Wells and his sister gave him a solid tombstone, so that he wasn't tempted to get up and wander off somewhere, in search of crocodiles.

A lot can happen in twenty years, and unfortunately not all of it gets recorded. 'Little Raki' is today a married man!

# Whispering in the Dark

A wild night. Wind moaning, trees lashing themselves in a frenzy, rain beating down on the road, thunder over the mountains. Loneliness stretched ahead of me, a loneliness of the heart as well as a physical loneliness. The world was blotted out by a mist that had come up from the valley, a thick, white, clammy shroud.

I groped through the forest, groped in my mind for the memory of a mountain path, some remembered rock or ancient deodar. Then a streak of blue lightning gave me a glimpse of a barren hillside and a house cradled in mist.

It was an old-world house, built of limestone rock on the outskirts of a crumbling hill station. There was no light in its windows; probably the electricity had been disconnected long ago. But if I could get in it would do for the night.

I had no torch, but at times the moon shone through the wild clouds, and trees loomed out of the mist like primeval giants. I reached the front door and found it locked from within. I walked round to the side and broke a windowpane, put my hand through shattered glass and found the bolt.

The window, warped by over a hundred monsoons, resisted at first. Then it yielded, and I climbed into the mustiness of a long-closed room, and the wind came in with me, scattering papers across the floor and knocking some unidentifiable object off a table. I closed the window, bolted it again, but the mist crawled through the broken glass, and the wind rattled in it like a pair of castanets.

There were matches in my pocket. I struck three before a light flared up.

I was in a large room, crowded with furniture. Pictures on the walls. Vases on the mantlepiece. A candlestand. And, strangely enough, no cobwebs. For all its external look of neglect and dilapidation, the house had been cared for by someone. But before I could notice anything else, the match burnt out.

As I stepped further into the room, the old deodar flooring creaked beneath my weight. By the light of another match I reached the mantlepiece and lit the candle, noticing at the same time that the candlestick was a genuine antique with cutglass hangings. A deserted cottage with good furniture and glass. I wondered why no one had ever broken in. And then realized that I had just done so.

I held the candlestick high and glanced round the room. The walls were hung with several watercolours and portraits in oils. There was no dust anywhere. But no one answered my call, no one responded to my hesitant knocking. It was as though the occupants of the house were in hiding, watching me obliquely from dark corners and chimneys.

I entered a bedroom and found myself facing a full-length

mirror. My reflection stared back at me as though I were a stranger, as though my reflection belonged to the house, while I was only an outsider.

As I turned from the mirror, I thought I saw someone, something, some reflection other than mine, move behind me in the mirror. I caught a glimpse of whiteness, a pale oval face, burning eyes, long tresses, golden in the candlelight. But when I looked in the mirror again there was nothing to be seen but my own pallid face.

A pool of water was forming at my feet. I set the candle down on a small table, found the edge of the bed—a large old four-poster—sat down, and removed my soggy shoes and socks. Then I took off my clothes and hung them over the back of a chair.

I stood naked in the darkness, shivering a little. There was no one to see me—and yet I felt oddly exposed, almost as though I had stripped in a room full of curious people.

I got under the bedclothes—they smelt slightly of eucalyptus and lavender—but found there was no pillow. That was odd. A perfectly made bed, but no pillow! I was too tired to hunt for one. So I blew out the candle—and the darkness closed in around me, and the whispering began...

The whispering began as soon as I closed my eyes. I couldn't tell where it came from. It was all around me, mingling with the sound of the wind coughing in the chimney, the stretching of old furniture, the weeping of trees outside in the rain.

Sometimes I could hear what was being said. The words came from a distance: a distance not so much of space as of time...

'Mine, mine, he is all mine....'

'He is ours, dear, ours.'

Whispers, echoes, words hovering around me with bats' wings, saying the most inconsequential things with a logical urgency. 'You're late for supper....'

'He lost his way in the mist.'

'Do you think he has any money?'

'To kill a turtle you must first tie its legs to two posts.'

'We could tie him to the bed and pour boiling water down his throat.'

'No, it's simpler this way.'

I sat up. Most of the whispering had been distant, impersonal, but this last remark had sounded horribly near.

I relit the candle and the voices stopped. I got up and prowled around the room, vainly looking for some explanation for the voices. Once again I found myself facing the mirror, staring at my own reflection and the reflection of that other person, the girl with the golden hair and shining eyes. And this time she held a pillow in her hands. She was standing behind me.

I remembered then the stories I had heard as a boy, of two spinster sisters—one beautiful, one plain—who lured rich, elderly gentlemen into their boarding house and suffocated them in the night. The deaths had appeared quite natural, and they had got away with it for years. It was only the surviving sister's death-bed confession that had revealed the truth—and even then no one had believed her.

But that had been many, many years ago, and the house had long since fallen down...

When I turned from the mirror, there was no one behind

me. I looked again, and the reflection had gone.

I crawled back into the bed and put the candle out. And I slept and dreamt (or was I awake and did it really happen?) that the woman I had seen in the mirror stood beside the bed, leant over me, looked at me with eyes flecked by orange flames. I saw people moving in those eyes. I saw myself. And then her lips touched mine, lips so cold, so dry, that a shudder ran through my body.

And then, while her face became faceless and only the eyes remained, something else continued to press down upon me, something soft, heavy and shapeless, enclosing me in a suffocating embrace. I could not turn my head or open my mouth. I could not breathe.

I raised my hands and clutched feebly at the thing on top of me. And to my surprise it came away. It was only a pillow that had somehow fallen over my face, half suffocating me while I dreamt of a phantom kiss.

I flung the pillow aside. I flung the bedclothes from me. I had had enough of whispering, of ownerless reflections, of pillows that fell on me in the dark. I would brave the storm outside rather than continue to seek rest in this tortured house.

I dressed quickly. The candle had almost guttered out. The house and everything in it belonged to the darkness of another time; I belonged to the light of day.

I was ready to leave. I avoided the tall mirror with its grotesque rococo design. Holding the candlestick before me, I moved cautiously into the front room. The pictures on the walls sprang to life.

One, in particular, held my attention, and I moved closer to examine it more carefully by the light of the dwindling candle. Was it just my imagination, or was the girl in the portrait the woman of my dream, the beautiful pale reflection in the mirror? Had I gone back in time, or had time caught up with me? Is it time that's passing by, or is it you and I?

I turned to leave, and the candle gave one final sputter and went out, plunging the room in darkness. I stood still for a moment, trying to collect my thoughts, to still the panic that came rushing upon me. Just then there was a knocking on the door.

'Who's there?' I called.

Silence. And then, again, the knocking, and this time a voice, low and insistent: 'Please let me in, please let me in....'

I stepped forward, unbolted the door, and flung it open.

She stood outside in the rain. Not the pale, beautiful one, but a wizened old hag with bloodless lips and flaring nostrils and—but where were the eyes? No eyes, no eyes!

She swept past me on the wind, and at the same time I took advantage of the open doorway to run outside, to run gratefully into the pouring rain, to be lost for hours among the dripping trees, to be glad for all the leeches clinging to my flesh.

And when, with the dawn, I found my way at last, I rejoiced in birdsong and the sunlight piercing and scattering the clouds.

And today if you were to ask me if the old house is still there or not, I would not be able to tell you, for the simple reason that I haven't the slightest desire to go looking for it.

# My Far Pavilions

*Bright red*
*The poinsettia flames,*
*As autumn and the old year wanes.*

When I have time on my hands, I write haikus, like the one above. This one brings back memories and images of my maternal grandmother's home in Dehra Dun, in the early 1940s. I say grandmother's home because, although grandfather built the house, he had passed on while I was still a child and I have no memories of him that I can conjure up. But he was someone about whom everyone spoke, and I learnt that he had personally supervised the building of the house, partially designing it on the lines of a typical Indian Railways bungalow—neat, compact, and without any frills. None of those Doric pillars, Gothic arches, and mediaeval turrets that characterized some of the Raj house for an earlier period. But instead of the customary red bricks, he used the smooth rounded stones from a local river bed, and this gave the bungalow a distinctive look.

In all the sixty-five years that I have lived in India, my grandparents' abode was the only house that gave me a feeling of some permanence, as neither my parents nor I were ever to own property. But India was my home, and it was big enough.

Grandfather looked after the mango and lichi orchard at the back of the house, grandmother looked after the flower garden in front. English flowers predominated—philox, larkspur, petunias, sweet peas, snapdragons, nasturtiums; but there was also a jasmine bush, poinsettias, and of course, lots of colourful bougainvillaea climbing the walls. And there were roses brought over from nearby Saharanpur. Saharanpur had become a busy railway junction and an industrial town, but its roses were still famous. It was the home of the botanical survey in northern India, and in the previous century many famous botanists and explorers had ventured into the Himalayas using Saharanpur as their base.

Grandfather had retired from the Railways and settled in Dehra around 1905. At this period, the small foothills town was becoming quite popular as a retreat for retiring Ango-Indian and domiciled Europeans. The bungalows had large compounds and gardens, and Dehra was to remain a garden town until a few years after Independence. The Forest Research Institute, the Survey of India, the Indian Military Academy, and a number of good schools, made the town a special sort of place. By the mid fifties, the pressures of population meant a greater demand for housing, and gradually the large compounds gave way to housing estates, and the gardens and orchards began to disappear. Most of the estates were now owned by the prospering Indian middle classes. Some of them strove to maintain the town's character and unique charm—flower shows, dog shows, school fetes, club life, dances, garden parties—but gradually these diminished; and today, as the capital of the new state of Uttaranchal, Dehra is as busy, congested and glamorous as any northern town or New Delhi suburb.

My father was always on the move. As a young man, he had been a schoolteacher at Lovedale, in the Nilgiris, then an assistant manager on a tea estate in Travancore-Cochin (now Kerala). He had also worked in the Ichhapore Rifle Factory bordering Calcutta. At the time I was born, he was employed in the Kathiawar states, setting up little schools for the state children in Jamnagar, Pithadia and Jetpur. I grew up in a variety of dwellings, ranging from leaky uid dak bungalows to spacious palace guesthouses. Then, during the Second World War, when he enlisted and was posted in Delhi, we moved from tent to Air Force hutment, to it flat in Scindia House, to rented rooms on Halley Road, Atul Grove, and elsewhere! When he was posted to Karachi, and then Calcutta, I was sent to boarding school in Shimla.

Father had, in fact, grown up in Calcutta, and his mother still lived at 14, Park Lane. She outlived all her children and continued to live at Park Lane until she was almost ninety. Last year, when I visited Calcutta, I found the Park Lane house. But it was boarded up. Nobody seemed to live there any more. Garbage was piled up near the entrance. A billboard hid most of the house from the road.

Possibly my boarding school, Bishop Cotton's in Shimla, provided me with a certain feeling of permanence, especially after I lost my father in 1944. Known as the 'Eton of the East', and run on English public school lines, Bishop Cotton's did not cater to individual privacy. Everyone knew what you kept in your locker. But when I became a senior, I was fortunate enough to be put in charge of the school library. I could use it in my free time, and it became my retreat, where I could read or write or just be on my own. No one bothered me there, for even in those pre-TV and pre-computer days there was no great demand for books! Reading was a minority pastime then, as it is now.

After school, when I was trying to write and sell my early short stories, I found myself ensconced in a tiny barsati, a room on the roof of all old lodging house in Dehra Dun. Alas! Granny's house had been sold by her eldest daugher, who had gone 'home' to England; my stepfather's home was full of half-brothers, stepbrothers and sundry relatives. The barsati gave me privacy.

A bed, a table and a chair were all that the room contained. It was all I needed. Even today, almost fifty years later, my room has the same basic furnishings, except that the table is larger, the bed is slightly more comfortable, and there is a rug on the floor, designed to trip me up whenever I sally forth from the room.

Then, as now, the view from the room, or from its windows, has always been an important factor in my life. I don't think I could stay anywhere for long unless I had a window from which to gaze out upon the world.

Dehra Dun isn't very far from where I live today, and I have passed granny's old bungalow quite often. It is really half a house now, a wall having been built through the centre of the compound. Like the country itself, it found itself partitioned, and there are two owners; one has the lichi trees and the other the mangoes. Good luck to both!

I do not venture in at the gate, I shall keep my memories intact. The only reminders of the past are a couple of potted geraniums on the verandah steps. And I shall sign off with another little haiku:

*Red geranium*
*Gleaming against the rain-bright floor...*
*Memory, hold the door!*

# A Knock at the Door

For Sherlock Holmes, it usually meant an impatient client waiting below in the street. For Nero Wolfe, it was the doorbell that rang, disturbing the great man in his orchid rooms. For Poe or Walter de la Mare, that knocking on a moonlit door could signify a ghostly visitor—no one outside!—or, even more mysterious, no one in the house...

Well, clients I have none, and ghostly visitants don't have to knock; but as I spend most of the day at home, writing, I have learnt to live with the occasional knock at the front door. I find doorbells even more startling than ghosts, and ornate brass knockers have a tendency to disappear when the price of brassware goes up; so my callers have to use their knuckles or fists on the solid mahogany door. It's a small price to pay for disturbing me.

I hear the knocking quite distinctly, as the small front room adjoins my even smaller study-cum-bedroom. But sometimes I keep up a pretense of not hearing anything straight away. Mahogany is good for the knuckles! Eventually, I place a pencil between my teeth and holding a sheet of blank foolscap in one hand, move slowly and thoughtfully toward the front door, so that, when I open it, my caller can see that I have been disturbed in the throes of composition. Not that I have ever succeeded in making any one feel guilty about it; they stay as long as they like. And after they have gone, I can get back to listening to my tapes of old Hollywood operettas.

Impervious to both literature and music, my first caller is usually a boy from the village, wanting to sell me his cucumbers or 'France-beans'. For some reason he won't call them French beans. He is not impressed by the accoutrements of my trade. He thrusts a cucumber into my arms and empties, the beans on a coffee-table book which has been sent to me for review. (There is no coffee table, but the book makes a good one.) He is confident that I cannot resist his France-beans, even though this sub-Himalayan variety is extremely hard and stringy. Actually, I am a sucker for cucumbers, but I take the beans so I can get the cucumber cheap. In this fashion, authors survive.

The deal done, and the door closed, I decide it's time to do some work. I start this little essay. If it's nice and gets published, I will be able to take care of the electricity bill. There's a knock at the door. Some knocks I recognize, but this is a new one. Perhaps it's someone asking for a donation. Cucumber in hand, I stride to the door and open it abruptly only to be confronted by a polite, smart-looking chauffeur who presents me with a large bouquet of flowering gladioli!

'With the compliments of Mr B.P. Singh,' he announces, before departing smartly with a click of the heels. I start looking for a receptacle for the flowers, as Grandmother's flower vase was really designed for violets and forget-me-nots.

B.P. Singh is a kind man who had the original idea of turning his property outside Mussoorie into a gladioli farm. A bare hillside is now a mass of gladioli from May to September. He sells them to flower shops in Delhi, but his heart bleeds at harvesting time.

Gladioli arranged in an ice bucket, I return to my desk and am just wondering what I should be writing next, when there is a loud banging on the door. No friendly knock this time. Urgent, peremptory, summoning! Could it be the police? And what have I gone and done? Every good citizen has at least one guilty secret, just waiting to be discovered! I move warily to the door and open it an inch or two. It is a policeman!

Hastily, I drop the cucumber and politely ask him if I can be of help. Try to look casual, I tell myself. He has a small packet in his hands. No, it's not a warrant. It turns out to be a slim volume of verse, sent over by a visiting DIG of Police, who has authored it. I thank his emissary profusely, and, after he has gone, I place the volume reverently on my bookshelf, beside the works of other poetry-loving policemen. These men of steel, who inspire so much awe and trepidation in the rest of us, they too are humans and some of them are poets!

Now it's afternoon, and the knock I hear is a familiar one, and welcome, for it heralds the postman. What would writers do without postmen? They have more power than literary agents. I don't have an agent (I'll be honest and say an agent won't have me), but I do have a postman, and he turns up every day except when there's a landslide.

Yes, it's Prakash the postman who makes my day, showering

me with letters, books, acceptances, rejections, and even the occasional cheque. These postmen are fine fellows, they do their utmost to bring the good news from Ghent to Aix.

And what has Prakash brought me today? A reminder: I haven't paid my subscription to the Author's Guild. I'd better send it off, or I shall be a derecognized author. A letter from a reader: would I like to go through her 800-page dissertation on the Gita? Some day, my love... A cheque, a cheque! From Sunflower Books, for nineteen rupees only, representing the sale of six copies of one of my books during the previous year. Never mind. Six wise persons put their money down for my book. No fresh acceptances, but no rejections either. A postcard from Goa, where one of my publishers is taking a holiday. So the post is something of an anti-climax. But I mustn't complain. Not every knock on the door brings gladioli fresh from the fields. Tomorrow's another day, and the postman comes six days a week.

# The Year of the Kissing and Other Good Times

'Seeds of the potato-berries should be sown in adapted places by explorers of new countries.'

So declared a botanically-minded empire-builder. And among those who took this advice was Captain Young of the Sirmur Rifles, Commandant of the Doon from the end of the Gurkha War in 1815 to the time of the Mutiny (1857).

It has to be said that the good captain was motivated by self-interest. He was an Irishman and fond of potatoes. He liked his Irish stew. So he grew his own potatoes and encouraged the good people of Garhwal to grow them too. In 1823, he received a supply of superior Irish potatoes and was considering where to plant them. The northern hill districts had been in British hands for almost ten years, but as yet no one had thought of resorting to them for rest or relaxation. The hills of central India, covered with jungle, were known to be extremely unhealthy. The Siwaliks near Dehra Dun were malarious. It was supposed that the Himalayan foothills, also forest clad, would be equally unhealthy. But Captain Young was to discover otherwise.

Carrying his beloved Irish potatoes with him, Captain Young set out on foot and soon left the sub-tropical Doon behind him. Above 4,000 feet he came to forests of oak and rhododendron, and above 6,000 feet they found cedars, known in the Himalayas as deodars or devdars—trees of the gods. He found a climate so cool and delightful that not only did he plant potatoes, he built himself a small hunting lodge facing the snows.

Captain Young was to make a number of visits to his little hut on the mountain. No one lived nearby. The villages were situated in the valleys, where water was available. Bears, leopards and wild boar roamed the forests. There were pheasants in the shady ravines and small trout in the little Aglar river. Young and his companions could hunt and fish to their hearts content. In 1826 Young, now a Colonel, built the first large house, 'Mullingar' (I see its remnants from my window every morning), on the way up to what became the convalescent depot and cantonment. Others soon began to follow Young's example, settling as far away as Cloud End and The Abbey. By 1830, the twin hill stations of Landour and Mussoorie had come into being.

Those early pleasure-seeking residents took little or no interest in potato growing, but Young certainly did, and the slope beneath his house became known as Colonel Young's potato field. You won't find potatoes there now, only Professor Saili's dahlias and cucumbers; but potato growing had caught on with the farmers in the surrounding villages, and soon everyone in Garhwal and beyond was growing potatoes.

The potato, practically unknown in India before its introduction in the nineteenth century, was soon to become a popular and vital ingredient of so many Indian dishes. The humble aloo made life much more interesting for chefs, housewives, gourmands and gourmets. The writers of cookery books would have a hard time filling out their pages without the help of the potato.

For aloo-mutter and aloo-dhum,

Our heartfelt thanks to Captain Young!

Shimla became the capital of British India, Nainital the capital of the United Provinces. These towns were soon teeming with officials and empire-builders. But Mussoorie remained non-official, the pleasure capital of the princes, wealthy Indians, European entrepreneurs, and the wives and mistresses of all of them. Mussoorie was smaller than Shimla, all length and not much width, but there was room enough for private lives, for discreet affairs conducted over picnic baskets beneath the whispering deodars.

Ah, those picnics! They seem to be a thing of the past, now that you can drive almost anywhere and find a line of dhabas awaiting you. Few people today bother to prepare those delicate sandwiches or delicious parathas when packets of potato chips and other fast foods are to be found at every bend of the road. Stop at any dhaba in the hills and an instant meal of chow mein will be ready for you. Professor Saili tells me that chow mein is now the national dish of Uttaranchal. I believe him. My own family members demand it whenever we are out for the day.

But to return to Mussoorie's easy-going early days, before

the missionaries arrived and made their own rules, imposing their ideas of morality upon the inhabitants.

The station's reputation was well established as far back as October 1884, when the local correspondent of the Calcutta *Statesman* wrote to his paper: 'Last Sunday, a sermon was delivered by the Rev Mr Hackett, belonging to the Church Mission society; he chose for his text Ezekiel 18th and 2nd verse, the latter clause: 'The fathers have eaten sour grapes and set their children's teeth on edge.' The reverend gentleman discoursed upon the highly immoral tone of society up here, that it far surpassed any other hill station in the scale of morals; that ladies and gentlemen after attending church proceeded to a drinking shop, a restaurant adjoining the library and there indulged freely in pegs, not one but many; that at a Fancy Bazaar held this season, a lady stood up on a chair and offered her kisses to gentlemen at Rs 5 each. What would they think of such a state of society at Home? But this was not all. 'Married ladies and married gents formed friendships and associations, which tended to no good purpose, and set a bad example.'

Adultery under the pines? Mussoorie was well ahead of the times. The poor reverend preached to no purpose. And it was just as well that he was not alive in the year 1933, when a lady stood up at a benefit show and auctioned a single kiss, for which a gentleman paid Rs 300, a substantial amount seventy years ago. (A year's house rent, in fact.) The *Statesman*'s correspondent had nothing to say on this latter occasion; his silence was in itself a comment on the changing times.

A few years ago I received a letter from a reader in England, wanting to know if there were any Maxwells still living in

Mussoorie. He was a Maxwell himself, he said, by his father's first marriage. From what he knew of the family history, there ought to have been several Maxwells by the second marriage, and he wanted to get in touch with them.

He was very frank and mentioned that his father had given up a brilliant career in the Indian Civil Service to marry a fourteen-year-old Muslim girl. He had met her in Madras, changed his religion to facilitate the marriage, and then—to avoid 'scandal'—had made his home with her in Mussoorie.

Although there are no longer any Maxwells living in Mussoorie, my former neighbour, Miss Bean, confirmed that Mr Maxwell's children from his second wife had grown up on the hillside, each inheriting a considerable property. The children emigrated, but one granddaughter returned to Mussoorie not so long ago, on a honeymoon with her fourth husband, thus keeping up the family tradition.

Mussoorie was probably at its brightest and gayest in the Thirties. Ballrooms, skating rinks and cinema halls flourished. Beauty saloons sprang up along the Mall. An old advertisement in my possession announces the superiority of Madame Freda in the art of 'permanent waving'. Another old ad recommends Holloway's Ointment as a 'certain remedy for bad legs, bad breasts, and ulcerations of all kinds.'

Darlington's Pain-Curer was another certain remedy for all manner of ailments. It was even recommended by His Highness Raja Pratap Sah of Tehri-Garhwal State, whose domains bordered Mussoorie: 'It affords me much pleasure in informing you that the two bottles of Darlington's Pain-Curer, which I took from you, has given extraordinary relief from the rheumatism I have been suffering since last six months. Therefore I request you to send me two bottles more (large size) as I wish to take this valuable medicine with me on my tour through the Himalaya mountains.'

Neither the ad nor his Highness tells us whether you were supposed to apply the potion or drink the stuff. Perhaps you could do both.

By the time Independence came to India, most of the British and Anglo-Indian residents of our hill stations had sold their homes and left the country. Only a few stayed on—elderly folks like Miss Bean who had spent all their lives here and whose meagre incomes did not allow them to settle abroad.

I wonder what really brought me to Mussoorie in the 1960s. True, I had been here as a child, and my mother's people had lived in Dehra Dun, in the valley below. When I returned to India, still a young man in my twenties (I had spent only four years in England), I lived in Delhi and Dehra Dun for a few years; and then, on an impulse, I found myself revisiting the hill station, calling on the oldest resident, Miss Bean, and being told by her that the upper portion of her cottage, Maplewood, was to let. On another impulse, I rented it.

Always a creature of impulse, my life has been shaped more by a benign providence than by any system of foresight or planning.

Well, that was forty years ago, and Miss Bean has long since gone to her Maker, and here I am in the midst of a large family, living in another cottage and doing my best to keep it from falling down.

Perhaps I really wanted to come back to my beginnings.

Because it was in Mussoorie in 1933 (the Year of the Kissing!) that my parents met each other and were married.

I have a photograph of them, on horseback, riding on the Camel's Back Road. He was thirty-six then and had just given up a tea-estate manager's job; she was barely twenty, taking a nurse's training at the Cottage Hospital, just below Gun Hill. A few months later they were living in the heat and dust of Alwar, in Rajasthan, and then Jamnagar in Kathiawar, where my father conducted a small palace school. I was not born in Mussoorie but I am pretty sure I had my conception there!

There is something in the air of the place—especially in October—that is conducive to love and passion and desire. Miss Bean told me that as a girl she'd many suitors, and if she did not marry it was more from procrastination than from being passed over. While on all sides elopements and broken marriages were making hill station life exciting, and providing orphans and illegitimate children for the mission schools, Miss Bean contrived to remain single and childless. She was probably helped by the fact of her father being a retired police officer with a reputation for being a good shot with the pistol and Lee-Enfield rifle.

She taught elocution in one of the many schools that flourished (and still flourish) in Mussoorie. There is a protective atmosphere about a residential school, an atmosphere which, although it protects one from the outside would, often exposes one to the hazards within the system.

The schools were not without their own scandals. Mrs Fennimore, the wife of a headmaster at Oak Grove, got herself entangled in a defamation suit, each hearing of which grew more and more distasteful to her husband. Unable to stand the whole weary and sordid business, Mr Fennimore hit upon a solution. Loading his revolver, he moved to his wife's bedside and shot her through the head. For no accountable reason he put the weapon under her pillow—obviously no one could have mistaken the death for suicide—and then, going to his study, he leaned over his rifle and shot himself.

Ten years later, in the same school, another headmaster's wife was arrested for attempted murder. She had fired at, and wounded a junior mistress. The motive remained obscure and the case was hushed up.

In the St. Fidelis' School, circa 1941, a boy asleep in the dormitory had his throat slit by another boy, it was said at the instigation of one of the teachers. This too was hushed up, but the school closed down a year later.

In recent years, there has been a suicide in one public school, and murders (involving students) in two others; also an accidental death by way of a drug overdose. Tom Brown's school days were pretty dull when compared to the goings on in some of our residential schools.

These affairs usually get hushed up, but there was no hushing up the incidents that took place on the 25 July 1927, at the height of the season and in the heart of the town—a double tragedy that set the station agog with excitement. It all happened in broad daylight and in a full boarding house, Zephyr Hall.

Shortly after noon the boarders were startled into brisk activity when a shot rang out from one of the rooms, followed by screams. Other shots followed in quick succession. Those boarders who happened to be in the lounge or on the verandah dived for the safety of their own rooms and bolted the doors. One unhappy boarder however, ignorant of where the man with the gun might be, decided to take no chances and came round the corner with his hands held well above his head only to run straight into the levelled pistol! Even the man who held it, and who had just shot his wife and daughter, couldn't help laughing.

Mr Owen, the maniac with the gun, after killing his wife and wounding his daughter finally shot himself. His was the first official Christian cremation in Mussoorie, performed apparently in compliance with wishes expressed long before his dramatic end.

A couple of years ago I had a letter from an old Mussoorie resident, Col. Cole, now retired in Pune, who recalled the event: 'Mrs Owen ran Zephyr Hall as a boarding house. It was the last Saturday of the month, and Mrs Owen's son Basil was with me at the 11 a.m.–1 p.m. session at the skating rink and so escaped the tragedy that took place about midday, when Mr Owen shot Mrs Owen and one daughter and then shot himself. I do not know what happened to Basil but he was withdrawn from school and an uncle took him over. This was not the end of the family tragedy. An older sister of Basil's in her early twenties was boating on the river Gumpti at Lucknow with her fiance, when a flash flood took place and the strong current drowned them both.'

This was not the end of the story, at least not for me.

A few summers ago, while I was walking along the Mall, I was stopped by a stranger, a small man with pale blue eyes and thinning hair. He must have been over sixty. Accompanying him was a much younger woman, whom he introduced as his wife.

He apologized for detaining me, and said: 'You look as though you have been here a long time. Do you know if any of the Gantzers still live here? I believe they look after the cemetery.'

I gave him the necessary directions and then asked him if he was visiting Mussoorie for the first time. He seemed to welcome the inquiry and showed a willingness to talk.

'It's well over fifty years since I was last here', he said. 'I was just a boy at the time'. And he gestured towards the ruins of Zephyr Hall, now occupied by postmen and their families. 'That was my mother's boarding house. That was where she died...'

'Not-not Mr Owen?' I ventured to ask.

'That's right. So you've heard about it. My father had a sudden brainstorm. He shot and killed Mother. My sister was badly wounded. I was out at the time. Now I have come to revisit her grave. I know she'd have wanted me to come.'

He took my telephone number and promised to look me up before he left Mussoorie. But I did not see him again. After a few days, I began to wonder if I had really met a survivor of this old tragedy, or if he had been just another of the hill station's ghosts. But one day, while I was walking along the cemetery's lowest terrace, I found confirmation that Mrs Owens son had indeed visited his mother's grave. Set into the tombstone was a new stone plaque with the inscription: *'Mother Dear, I am Here.'*

# A Hill Station's Vintage Murders

There is less crime in the hills than in the plains, and so the few murders that do take place from time to time stand out as landmarks in the annals of a hill station.

Among the gravestones in the Mussoorie cemetery there is one which bears the inscription: 'Murdered by the hand he befriended.' This is the grave of Mr James Reginald Clapp, a chemist's assistant, who was brutally done to death on the night of 31 August 1909.

Miss Ripley-Bean, who has spent most of her eighty-seven years in this hill station, remembers the case clearly, though she was only a girl at the time. From the details she has given me, and from a brief account in *A Mussoorie Miscellany*, now out of print, I am able to reconstruct this interesting case and a couple of others which were the sensations of their respective 'seasons'.

Mr Clapp was an assistant in the chemist's shop of Messrs. J.B. & E. Samuel (no longer in existence), situated in one of the busiest sections of the Mall. At that time the adjoining cantonment of Landour was an important convalescent centre for British soldiers. Mr Clapp was popular with the soldiers, and he had befriended some of them when they had run short of money. He was a steady worker and sent most of his savings home, to his mother in Birmingham; she was planning to use the money to buy the house in which she lived.

At the time of the murder, Clapp was particularly friendly with a Corporal Allen, who was eventually to be hanged at the Naini Jail. The murder was brutal, the initial attack being launched with a soda-water bottle on the victim's head. Clapp's throat was then cut from ear to ear with his own razor, which was left behind in the room. The body was discovered on the floor of the shop the next morning by the proprietor, Mr Samuel, who did not live on the premises.

Suspicion immediately fell on Corporal Allen because he had left Mussoorie that same night, arriving at Rajpur, in the foothills (a seven-mile walk by the bridle path) many hours later than he was expected at a Rajpur boarding house. According to some, Clapp had last been seen in the corporal's company.

There was other circumstantial evidence pointing to Allen's guilt. On the day of the murder, Mr Clapp had received his salary, and this sum, in sovereigns and notes, was never traced. Allen was alleged to have made a payment in sovereigns at Rajpur. Someone had given Allen a biscuit tin packed with sandwiches for his journey down, and it was thought that perhaps the tin had been used by the murderer as a safe for the money. But no tin was found, and Allen denied having had one with him.

Allen was arrested at Rajpur and brought back to Mussoorie under escort. He was taken immediately to the victim's bedside, where the body still lay, the police hoping that he might confess his guilt when confronted with the body of the victim; but Allen was unmoved, and protested his innocence.

Meanwhile, other soldiers from among Mr Clapp's friends had collected on the Mall. They had removed their belts and were ready to lynch Allen as soon as he was brought out of the shop. The situation was tense, but further mishap was averted by the resourcefulness of Mr Rust, a photographer, who, being of the same build as the corporal, put on an army coat with a turned-up collar, and arranged to be handcuffed between two policemen. He remained with them inside the shop, in partial view of the mob, while the rest of the police party escorted the corporal out by a back entrance. Mr Rust did not abandon his disguise or leave the shop until word arrived that Allen was secure in the police station.

Corporal Allen was eventually found guilty, and was hanged. But there were many who felt that he had never really been proved guilty, and that he had been convicted on purely circumstantial evidence; and looking back on the case from this distance in time one cannot help feeling that the soldier may have been a victim of circumstances, and perhaps of local prejudice, for he was not liked by his fellows. Allen himself hinted that he was not in the vicinity of the crime that night but in the company of a lady whose integrity he was determined to shield. If this was true, it was a pity that the lady prized her virtue more than her friend's life, for she did not come forward to save him. The chaplain who administered to Allen during his last days in the 'condemned cell' was prepared to absolve the corporal and could not accept that he was a murderer.

One of the hill station's most sensational crimes was

committed on 25 July 1927, at the height of the 'season' and in the heart of the town, in Zephyr Hall, then a boarding house. It provided a good deal of excitement for the residents of the boarding house.

Soon after midday, Zephyr Hall residents were startled into brisk activity when a woman screamed and a shot rang out from one of the rooms. Other shots followed in rapid succession.

Those boarders who happened to be in the public lounge or verandah dived for the safety of their rooms; but one unhappy resident, taking the precaution of coming around a corner with his hands held well above his head, ran straight into a levelled pistol. And the man with the gun, who had just killed his wife and wounded his daughter, was still able to see some humour in the situation, for he burst into laughter! The boarder escaped unhurt. But the murderer, Mr Owen, did not savour the situation for long. He shot himself long before the police arrived.

Ten years earlier, on 24 November 1917, another husband had shot his wife.

Mrs Fennimore, the wife of a schoolmaster, had got herself inextricably enmeshed in a defamation law suit, each hearing of which was more distasteful to Mr Fennimore than the previous one. Finally he determined on his own solution. Late at night he armed himself with a loaded revolver, moved to his wife's bedside, and, finding her lying asleep on her side, shot her through the back of the head. For no accountable reason he put the weapon under her pillow, and then completed his plan. Going to the lavatory, three rooms beyond his wife's bedroom, he leaned over his loaded rifle and shot himself.

# The Garlands on His Brow

*Fame has but a fleeting hold*
*On the reins in our fast-paced society;*
*So many of yesterday's heroes crumble.*

Shortly after my return from England, I was walking down the main road of my old hometown of Dehra, gazing at the shops and passers-by to see what changes, if any, had taken place during my absence. I had been away three years. Still a boy when I went abroad, I was twenty-one when I returned with some mediocre qualifications to flaunt in the faces of my envious friends (I did not tell them of the loneliness of those years in exile; it would not have impressed them). I was nearing the clock tower when I met a beggar coming from the opposite direction. In one respect, Dehra had not changed. The beggars were as numerous as ever, though I must admit they looked healthier.

This beggar had a straggling beard, a hunch, a cavernous chest and unsteady legs on which a number of purple sores were festering. His shoulders looked as though they had once been powerful, and his hands thrusting a begging bowl at me, were still strong.

He did not seem sufficiently decrepit to deserve my charity, and I was turning away when I thought I discerned a gleam recognition in his eyes. There was something slightly familiar about the man; perhaps he was a beggar who remembered me from earlier years. He was even attempting a smile; showing me a few broken yellow fangs; and to get away from him, I produced a coin, dropped it in his bowl and hurried away.

I had gone about a hundred yards when, with a rush of memory, I knew the identity of the beggar. He was the hero of my childhood. Hassan, the most magnificent wrestler in the entire district.

I turned and retraced my steps, half hoping I wouldn't be able catch up with the man and he had indeed got lost in the bazaar crowd. Well, I would doubtless be confronted by him again in a day or two... Leaving the road, I went into the municipal gardens and stretching myself out on the fresh green February grass, allowed my memory to journey back to the days when I was a boy of ten, full of health and optimism, when my wonder at the great game of living had yet to give way to disillusionment at its shabbiness.

On those precious days when I played truant from school— and I would have learnt more had I played truant more often—I would sometimes make my way to the akhara at the corner of the gardens to watch the wrestling pit. My chin cupped in my hands, I would lean against a railing and gaze in awe at the rippling muscles, applauding with the other watchers whenever one of the wrestlers made a particularly clever move or pinned an opponent down on his back.

Amongst these wrestlers the most impressive and engaging young man was Hassan, the son of a kite maker. He had a magnificent build, with great wide shoulders and powerful legs, and what he lacked in skill he made up for in sheer animal strength and vigour. The idol of all small boys, he was followed about by large numbers of us, and I was a particular favourite of his. He would offer to lift me on to his shoulders and carry me across the akhara to introduce me to his friends and fellow wrestlers.

From being Dehra's champion, Hassan soon became the outstanding representative of his art in the entire district. His technique improved, he began using his brain in addition to his brawn, and it was said by everyone that he had the makings of a national champion.

It was during a large fair towards the end of the rains that destiny took a hand in the shaping of his life. The Rani of—was visiting the fair, and she stopped to watch the wrestling bouts. When she saw Hassan stripped and in the ring, she began to take more than a casual interest in him. It has been said that she was a woman of a passionate and amoral nature, who could not be satisfied by her weak and ailing husband. She was struck by Hassan's perfect manhood, and through an official offered him the post of her personal bodyguard.

The Rani was rich and, in spite of having passed her fortieth summer, was a warm and attractive woman. Hassan did not find it difficult to make love according to the bidding, and on the whole he was happy in her service. True, he did not wrestle as often as in the past; but when he did enter a competition, his reputation and his physique combined to overawe his opponents, and they did not put up much resistance. One or two well-known wrestlers were invited to the district. The Rani paid them liberally, and they permitted Hassan to throw them out of the ring. Life in the Rani's house was comfortable and easy, and Hassan, a simple male, felt himself secure. And it is to the credit of the Rani (and also of Hassan) that she did not tire of him as quickly as she had of others.

But ranis, like washerwomen, are mortal; and when a long-standing and neglected disease at last took its toll, robbing her at once of all her beauty, she no longer struggled against it, but allowed it to poison and consume her once magnificent body. It would be wrong to say that Hassan was heartbroken when she died. He was not a deeply emotional or sensitive person. Though he could attract the sympathy of others, he had difficulty in producing any of his own. His was a kindly but not compassionate nature.

He had served the Rani well, and what he was most aware of now was that he was without a job and without any money. The Raja had his own personal amusements and did not want a wrestler who was beginning to sag a little about the waist.

Times had changed. Hassan's father was dead, and there was no longer a living to be had from making kites; so Hassan returned to doing what he had always done: wrestling. But there was no money to be made at the akhara. It was only in the professional arena that a decent living could be made. And so, when a travelling circus of professionals—a Negro, a Russian, a Cockney-Chinese and a giant Sikh—came to town and offered a hundred rupees and a contract to the challenger who could stay five minutes in the ring with any one of them, Hassan took up the challenge.

He was pitted against the Russian, a bear of a man, who wore a black mask across his eyes; and in two minutes Hassan's Dehra supporters saw their hero slung about the ring, kicked in the head and groin, and finally flung unceremoniously through the ropes.

After this humiliation, Hassan did not venture into competitive bouts again. I saw him sometimes at the akhara, where he made a few rupees giving lessons to children. He had a paunch, and folds were beginning to accumulate beneath his chin. I was no longer a small boy, but he always had a smile and a hearty backslap reserved for me.

I remember seeing him a few days before I went abroad. He was moving heavily about the akhara; he had lost the lightning swiftness that had once made him invincible. Yes, I told myself.

*The garlands wither on your brow;*
*They boast no more your mighty deeds...*

That had been over three years ago. And for Hassan to have been reduced to begging was indeed a sad reflection of both the passing of time and the changing times. Fifty years ago, a popular local wrestler would never have been allowed to fall into a state of poverty and neglect. He would have been fed by his old friends, and stories would have been told of his legendary prowess. He would not have been forgotten. But those were more leisurely times, when the individual had his place in society, when a man was praised for his past achievement, and his failures were tolerated and forgiven. But life had since become fast and cruel and unreflective, and people were too busy counting their gains to bother about the idols of their youth.

It was a few days after my last encounter with Hassan that I found a small crowd gathered at the side of the road, not far from the clock tower. They were staring impassively at something in the drain, at the same time keeping a discreet distance. Joining the group, I saw that the object of their disinterested curiosity was a corpse, its head hidden under a culvert, legs protruding into the open drain. It looked as though the man had crawled into the drain to die, and had done so with his head in the culvert so the world would not witness his last unavailing struggle.

When the municipal workers came in their van, and lifted the body out of the gutter, a cloud of flies and bluebottles rose from the corpse with an angry buzz of protest. The face was muddy, but I recognized the beggar who was Hassan.

In a way, it was a consolation to know that he had been forgotten, that no one present could recognize the remains of the man who had once looked like a young god. I did not come forward to identify the body. Perhaps I saved Hassan from one final humiliation.

# Death of the Trees

The peace and quiet of the Maplewood hillside disappeared forever one winter. The powers that be decided to build another new road into the mountains, and the PWD saw fit to take it right past the cottage, about six feet from the large window which had overlooked the forest.

In my journal I wrote:

Already they have felled most of the trees. The walnut was one of the first to go. A tree I had lived with for over ten years, watching it grow just as I had watched Prem's little son, Rakesh, grow up... Looking forward to its new leafbuds, the broad, green leaves of summer turning to spears of gold in September when the walnuts were ripe and ready to fall. I knew this tree better than the others. It was just below the window, where a buttress for the road is going up.

Another tree I'll miss is the young deodar, the only one growing in this stretch of the woods. Some years back it was stunted from lack of sunlight. The oaks covered it with their shaggy branches. So I cut away some of the overhanging branches and after that the deodar grew much faster. It was just coming into its own this year; now cut down in its prime like my young brother on the road to Delhi last month: both victims of the roads; the tree killed by the PWD, my brother by a truck.

Twenty oaks have been felled. Just in this small stretch near the cottage. By the time this bypass reaches Jabarkhet, about six miles from here, over a thousand oaks will have been slaughtered, besides many other fine trees—maples, deodars and pines—most of them unnecessarily, as they grow some fifty to sixty yards from the roadside.

The trouble is, hardly anyone (with the exception of the contractor who buys the felled trees) really believes that trees and shrubs are necessary. They get in the way so much, don't they? According to my milkman, the only useful tree is one which can be picked clean of its leaves for fodder! And a young man remarked to me: 'You should come to Pauri. The view is terrific, there are no trees in the way!'

Well, he can stay here now, and enjoy the view of the ravaged hillside. But as the oaks have gone, the milkman will have to look further afield for his fodder.

Rakesh calls the maples the butterfly trees because when the winged seeds fall they flutter like butterflies in the breeze. No maples now. No bright red leaves to flame against the sky. No birds!

That is to say, no birds near the house. No longer will it be possible for me to open the window and watch the scarlet minivets flitting through the dark green foliage of the oaks; the long-tailed magpies gliding through the trees; the barbet calling insistently from his perch on top of the deodar. Forest birds, all of them, they will now be in search of some other stretch of surviving forest. The only visitors will be the crows, who have learnt to live with, and off, humans and seem to multiply along with roads, houses and people. And even when all the people have gone, the crows will still be around.

Other things to look forward to: trucks thundering past in the night; perhaps a tea and pakora shop round the corner; the grinding of gears, the music of motor horns. Will the whistling thrush be heard above them? The explosions that continually shatter the silence of the mountains—as thousand-year-old rocks are dynamited—have frightened away all but the most intrepid of birds and animals. Even the bold langoors haven't shown their faces for over a fortnight.

Somehow, I don't think we shall wait for the tea shop to arrive. There must be some other quiet corner, possibly on the next mountain, where new roads have yet to come into being. No doubt this is a negative attitude, and if I had any sense I'd open my own tea shop. To retreat is to be a loser. But the trees are losers too; and when they fall, they do so with a certain dignity. Never mind. Men come and go; the mountains remain.

www.ingramcontent.com/pod-product-compliance
Lightning Source LLC
Chambersburg PA
CBHW030552030726
47495CB00004B/1221